"*The Nansen Factor* weaves a tapestry of lives uprooted and reshaped by the tides of history. From the stirring upheaval of the Bolshevik Revolution to the haunting memories of Paris and beyond, these interconnected stories traverse a century of exile, loss, and resilience. Each tale is a testament to the spirit of those who must forge new paths from the fragments of the past."

 —Sana Krasikov, author of *One More Year* and *The Patriots*

"Spanning the globe from St. Petersburg to Shanghai, Grabbe's stunning debut charts the interconnected lives of unmoored Russians and their descendants. *The Nansen Factor* dramatizes a century of love, loss, longing, brutality, and determination as experienced by a sweeping cast of characters, from poor migrants to aspiring actors to modern-day Americans haunted by the past. This is a riveting and essential collection."

 —Chip Cheek, author of *Cape May*

"*The Nansen Factor* opens us to the multitude of ways immigration trauma emerges in future generations. These are poignant stories of the opportunity and hardship of reclaiming lives in a new land. The fallacy of forgetting and the management of grief is a human predicament, and these moving stories are a testament to this shared humanity. Such an important message for our times!"

 —Laurel M. Silber, Psy.D.

"These poignant and beautifully crafted tales bring a human touch to the bittersweet experience of exile."

 —Anatol Shmelev, Hoover Institution, Stanford University

"Gorgeous prose, delicate storytelling that tags at the reader's heartstrings. The entire generation of White Russia, the first wave of Russian emigration, comes alive. This book gives personal scale to the vastness of their displacement around the globe. Engrossing, timely, and empathetic towards the victims of political upheaval."

—Yelena Lembersky, author of
Like a Drop of Ink in a Downpour

"*The Nansen Factor* is a spellbinding exploration of migration and exile, and the aftershocks that ripple through the generations. Alexandra Grabbe animates the impact of history's vast movements on individual lives in these insightful, elegant, and moving stories. This is a wonderful collection."

—Laura van den Berg, author of *State of Paradise*, *Find Me*,
and *Hold a Wolf by the Ears*

"The stories in this impressive collection beautifully express the enrichment and estrangement of displaced lives. With a single phrase or tiny detail, Grabbe accurately captures an entire soul and the fractured, complicated state of living between worlds. A bold and engrossing debut with unforgettable characters."

—Marjan Kamali, author of *The Stationery Shop*
and *Tiger Women of Tehran*

The

NANSEN
FACTOR

The

NANSEN
FACTOR

Refugee Stories

ALEXANDRA GRABBE

Boston 2024

Library of Congress Cataloging-in-Publication Data

Names: Grabbe, Alexandra, author.
Title: The Nansen factor: refugee stories / Alexandra Grabbe.
Description: Boston: Cherry Orchard Books, 2024.
Identifiers: LCCN 2024005687 (print) | LCCN 2024005688 (ebook) |
    ISBN 9798887195094 (paperback) | ISBN 9798887195100 (adobe
    pdf) | ISBN 9798887195117 (epub)
Subjects: LCSH: Soviet Union--History--Revolution, 1917-1921--Refugees
    --Fiction. | Russians--Foreign countries--Fiction. | Historical fiction,
    American. | LCGFT: Historical fiction. | Linked stories.
Classification: LCC PS3607.R24 N36 2024 (print) | LCC PS3607.R24
    (ebook) | DDC 813/.6--dc23/eng/20240306
LC record available at https://lccn.loc.gov/2024005687
LC ebook record available at https://lccn.loc.gov/2024005688

Library of Congress Control Number: 2024005687
Copyright © Alexandra Grabbe, 2024

ISBN 9798887195094 paperback
ISBN 9798887195100 Adobe PDF
ISBN 9798887195117 ePub

Book design by PHi Business Solutions
Cover design by Whitney Scharer. whitneyscharer.com

Published by Cherry Orchard Books, and imprint of Academic Studies Press
1577 Beacon St.
Brookline, MA 02446, USA
Tel: +1.617.782.6290

press@academicstudiespress.com
www.academicstudiespress.com

Grateful acknowledgement is made to the following publications where some of these stories originally appeared: "The Errand" in *Five on the Fifth;* "Out Of This Word" in *Fiction on the Web UK* and *The Offbeat;* "Shamil" in *The Gateway Review* and *Joining Forces,* an anthology from JayHenge Publishing; "Buried Treasure" in *New World Writing.*

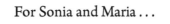

For Sonia and Maria . . .

Author's Note

Nansen passports—official passports created for stateless persons—were travel documents internationally recognized from 1922 to 1938. Norwegian diplomat Fridtjof Nansen became the first High Commissioner for Refugees at the League of Nations, a position he used to create these documents and help stateless refugees. He received the Nobel Peace Prize in 1922 for his work.

Contents

"If we are willing to listen, the history of disarticulated grief is still speaking through the living, and the future of social transformation depends on how open we are to facing the intricacies and paradoxes of that grief and the passions that it bequeaths."

—A. Cheng

"Immigrant resilience is built on forgetting and working towards a new start. What will the backward glance accomplish?"

—Svetlana Boym

The Errand

Waking up in an unfamiliar place gives me the willies so I think about home as I wait for the woodstove to remove the chill from my cousin's bedroom. It's a cold morning in mid-March 1917. We're going shopping today, for books. I'm a big fan of Arsène Lupin and Yuri says he knows where I can buy the French burglar's latest adventure to read on the train to Kislovodsk in Southern Russia.

I devour my share of breakfast—three sweet buns with butter. Yuri waves me over to the window and rubs the glass with his pajama sleeve. The matted frost clears enough to reveal the snow-covered Neva stretching to either side. Mist shrouds the opposite bank.

"What a view!" I exclaim.

"Over there to the right? That's the Cathedral of Peter and Paul."

Yes, I can make out the narrow spire, a golden needle that sparkles in the sunlight. Down on the river a few pedestrians stagger across the uneven ice, too lazy to walk to the bridge. Below us, a man trudges along the quay. His gloved hand trails on the granite wall, raising white puffs of snow.

Once we're dressed, Yuri hands me a tortoiseshell comb. I run the comb through my unruly locks, parting my hair in the middle with a dab of saliva. His expression remains unchanged although he must miss his long hair, gone due to military school regulations.

The valet gives Yuri a cap and leather gloves before help-ing him with his coat, a heavy black military overcoat. "The chauffeur didn't come today," Matvei says. He waddles along beside us, attempting to brush Yuri's lapels with a horsehair clothes brush.

"Which means Volodia and I have to take the streetcar?"

They make a funny pair: Matvei, short and stout, and Yuri who has shot up several inches since Christmas. Our fathers were brothers. Mine died five years ago. That's how I know life can change in an instant. I pay particular attention to the rest of their conversation.

"Maybe you and Vladimir Nikolaievich should stay home," Matvei is saying. "There might not be . . . it might not be safe."

"How's that? Unsafe?"

"Worse than unsafe. Dangerous. My carpenter friend came by last night, trying to get me to leave . . . you know, again. He said the revolution was supposed to start tomorrow. That means today. We can expect shooting in the streets."

"And you believed him?"

"Of course not."

"Well, I don't either." After a moment of hesitation, Yuri cocks his head toward the hallway, where I stand in front of the mirror. I'm ballooning out my cheek to examine the mole I hate so much. Also checking for pimples. "We're going on an errand. Volodia here needs a book."

With reluctance, Matvei pushes the door shut.

"Shouldn't we tell your mom?" I ask on the stairs.

Yuri breaks into a grin. "No need."

I envy his independence. Auntie lets him go out by him-self, and he's only eleven months older. Although I turned fourteen last month, I'm forbidden to go anywhere without a chaperone.

Outside, in the brisk morning air, I pull down the flaps of my otter skin cap and peer over my shoulder at the row of townhouses. Most of the blinds are drawn though it must be close to ten o'clock.

Yuri pivots to look back. "Seems normal. Onward."

I thrust my hands deep into my overcoat pockets. If Mum knew about our errand, she'd be horrified. She keeps repeating that there may be another revolt. That's why we're going south tomorrow.

"Pay no attention to Matvei," Yuri says as we approach the bridge. "He worries about me. Got a valet?"

"A tutor," I reply, lest he think we're unable to afford servants.

"I used to have a tutor. Now I attend the Corps des Pages."

"Mum says we can dispense with valets since we don't live in the city anymore."

Yuri's a good sort. From the way he narrows his eyes, I can tell he has remembered my mother is a widow and our circumstances no longer allow multiple servants. Mum has her lady's maid. She's like family. Matvei, too, obviously cares about Yuri. I hurry to catch up as he reaches the broad avenue leading to the city center.

We proceed in silence for a while. I ask how he likes military school. He says it's okay. I ask about his father, whether he's afraid for his future since he holds an important position at court according to Mum, another topic Yuri doesn't feel like discussing. I bring up hobbies. He collects postage stamps. I tell him I carve miniature boats out of bark.

At the streetcar stop, I stamp my feet on the rectangular platform to remove snow. I haven't spent much time in Petrograd since last fall when Mum made me attend cotillion. How I hated those dance lessons.

Yuri scans the bridge. "See any streetcars?"

I give my head a quick shake. Frost bites at my feet. That's when we hear a hum, and a streetcar careens around the corner. We step back as it thunders past.

"How odd," Yuri says. "What's going on?"

"Revolution?"

"Oh, I doubt it. A revolution means street fighting, noise, shooting. There's none of that."

The place is mournful. Not a sound. Like a cemetery. Across from where we stand, an alley breaks the line of low buildings. Yuri points at a rickety pushcart, abandoned by some fruit vendor. We move the heavy pushcart onto the rails.

The next streetcar's wheels make a high-pitched metallic whine once the conductor spots our barricade. While he clears away the debris, we climb aboard.

I stare out the window as the cityscape flies by. I've brought some wool to plug up my ears but hesitate to use it, afraid Yuri might make fun of me. I don't know him all that well. Our families only get together at Christmas and Easter.

We pass my sister's new flat, where Mum spent the night, hoping to convince Lisa to join us. Her husband and my brother are both at the Front. They consider military service as a means of advancement in life. Not me. I'd prefer to report on the war as a journalist, say, or write mysteries for children.

We're going fast, faster than necessary. Yuri gropes his way to the front of the swaying car.

"Excuse me, what's the rush?" He rings the bell several times. "Stop!" he shrieks. "Nevsky Prospect! Let us off."

The conductor slams his foot on the brake. "I'm trying to get out of the way. Nothing more, Comrade. And I would give you fair warning to do the same."

As we hop out, I make note of the red ribbon on his uniform. When my tutor described the worker strikes of 1905, he said white means surrender, black represents anarchy, and red stands for revolution. The conductor's insolence reminds me of the valet's warning. I gnaw the interior of my cheek, booted feet gripping the cobblestones, toes curved down, while the streetcar speeds away, rattling and shaking.

"Yuri, maybe this isn't such a good idea."

He responds with a light laugh, as much as to say not to worry.

The city center is crowded. Not only sleighs but highly polished automobiles glide by, making the crusted snow crackle. Some pedestrians chat, while others stride along muffled in fur. A gold-spectacled birdlike fellow with a neat beard and a doctor bag scurries past waving. Yuri tells me it's his family doctor, Anatoly Petrovich Sharin, who lives nearby. A merry company of men and women—actors?—emerge from a restaurant or it could be a nightclub. An elegant man with a goatee exchanges a few words with an *izvozchik*, leaning against his sleigh.

"*Niet, barin*," the driver says with a good-natured laugh. "One ruble? Have pity! I'd take you yonder for five kopeks. I would tomorrow, but not today."

Without a doubt, we've picked the wrong day for errands. I glance at Yuri.

"What do you think? Maybe we should head back."

He slaps his cheek in disbelief. "Do you want this book or not?!"

He's right. I'll be bored on the trip south with nothing to read.

My apprehension fades once inside the bookshop. It's warm and smells of peppermint. Leather-bound books are piled on the counter. I find the foreign books section and locate *813*, one of my all-time favorites, a mystery about how Arsène Lupin, accused of murder, gets disguised as a police investigator and clears himself by tracking down the real killer. I ask the shopkeeper for *The Golden Triangle*. He gives me this long explanation about the challenges involved in the import of foreign literature. During our conversation, it occurs to me that we are his only customers. He says his shipment may arrive later only he cannot guarantee the shop will be open. That we're welcome to return. I buy a fresh copy of *813* instead.

While we're crossing the bridge over the Fontanka, Yuri shades his eyes. I follow his gaze down the Nevsky. Half a dozen blocks away, shadows flit back and forth. Windows open as shots ring out. Couples cluster on balconies. Yuri quickens his pace.

"Whoa!" I shout after him, feeling more anxious by the minute since he's heading in the wrong direction. I'd be willing to go investigate if not for all the warnings we've had this morning. In fact, right now, I'd prefer to be home in bed or even at dance class. The most exciting thing that happens in our village is the birth of a foal. In fall, mushrooms pop up through the dead leaves after a heavy rain and our cook makes mushroom pies, enough to donate a couple to the local clergy.

"Yuri, we should go back to your house," I repeat when I catch up.

Too late. He has already opened a door and yanks me into a building. The lobby smells of cooked cabbage and the English Rose perfume Aunt Lila used to wear. A wall sign indicates Dr. Sharin receives patients on the second floor, but the receptionist there tells us he has gone upstairs to his home on the fourth floor. We dash up the spiral staircase and ring the doorbell three times. The doctor himself opens the door. He draws back and coughs twice, surprised at seeing us.

"Sorry to bother you," Yuri says, polite as can be. "Something out of the ordinary is happening on your street. Do you mind if we join you at the window?"

The front parlor is furnished with a deep-buttoned sofa, armchairs, a couple of lamps, and a plush oriental rug. Two large gold-framed landscapes with cows cover the wall above a highly carved credenza. Yuri throws open both windows. I take up position on the far side of the room, behind a fringed lampshade, relieved to be indoors. A breeze has thinned the mist, and the automobiles and sleighs have all but vanished. Dr. Sharin removes an ornate timepiece from his waistcoat to check the hour and shuffles off into a corridor, saying he'll fetch opera glasses.

The sky is luminous, with pearl-grey clouds dominant in the west. No doubt it will snow this afternoon. One corner of the windowsill wears a cuff of white, tinged with black specks. I stick my gloved finger in to break up the crystals and form a loose snowball, which I toss from hand to hand. In my mind, it's the dead of night. Arsène Lupin, dressed as a cat burglar, leaps onto the ledge to save a damsel in distress. I see myself at the foot of the building, steadying his ladder.

My daydream fades as a shot rings out, followed by two more. Pedestrians duck into doorways or crouch down low. Men have filled the Nevsky, shouting in strident voices, "Freedom! Revolution!" Some carry rifles with fixed bayonets. Many wear red armbands. The men raise a red flag that flashes with gold.

Below us, governmental troops march around the corner in formation and roll a machine gun toward the intersection. My heart is pounding. The soldiers seem to have arrived in the nick of time. We hear more shots, followed by a heavy burst of gunfire. An empty sleigh, pulled by a frantic horse, tears off toward the river.

"That must be a Maxim," Yuri calls to the doctor who has located his opera glasses and raises them to his eyes. "Can you believe the size of the thing?"

Dr. Sharin claws the windowsill with his left hand, still holding the opera glasses with the right. "Good lord," he gasps. "I do believe they intend to shoot people."

Pedestrians race down the street, leaping into doorways to avoid bullets. Some fall headlong, shot in the back. In awkward positions, they remain where they've fallen or crawl forward, arms outstretched. I squeeze my eyes shut and reopen them. A woman, wearing a veiled hat like the one Mum wore at Papa's funeral, clutches her breast as she stumbles to the ground. It's grotesque, like finding oneself in a painting by Hieronymus Bosch. I retreat a step and swallow hard. I can't believe people are dying.

Dr. Sharin collapses into an armchair, head in his hands.

Yuri snatches the opera glasses, fiddles with the focus. "Here, your turn," he says after a minute or two. "Hold them like this."

I follow orders, although I don't need opera glasses to realize our side is losing. The shabbily dressed men are ferocious fighters. There's a final mighty rush for the Maxim. Steadily, the governmental troops back away. A truck arrives. More revolutionaries leap out and hoist the gun onto its carriage. In no time they round the corner and disappear.

"Time to go." I push Yuri toward the door.

"Boys, wait," Dr. Sharin calls out. He removes a worn sheepskin coat and a leather cap trimmed with fur from a closet. "Put these on, Yuri Alexandrovich. It's probably not safe to walk around in military clothing."

We dive down the stairs, two by two, into the lobby, now filled with frightened people, a dozen at least, packed into the narrow space. The women cluck and groan about the shooting. A nanny tries to comfort a rosy-cheeked baby. A couple argues over who fired first.

"Coming through," someone yells. Two men carry in an elderly woman on a stretcher and start up the staircase. Gurgles come from her mouth.

"What kind of outfit are you masquerading in?"

Startled to have someone address us in such an aggressive manner, we both swing around to confront a young man who glares back at us, his black eyes half-closed as though he's a judge, and we're criminals.

"Foronov!" Yuri says with affected cheerfulness. "What a surprise. This is my cousin Volodia."

Foronov's clothes are immaculate. His nose, pinched by a pair of almond-shaped eyeglasses, is slightly puckered, and his dark eyebrows are drawn in an obvious attempt to look severe. He wears his military cap tilted forward in accordance with the latest fashion. Its top, both circular and stiff, resembles a dried pancake. The tsar's initials glisten on the golden epaulettes, as do the metal buttons of his long black overcoat. I recognize his swagger. My brother adopted the same attitude in his last years at the Corps des Pages. The tsar's initials were sewn onto the shoulders of his uniform. Nika was incredibly proud of those epaulettes.

Foronov readjusts his eyeglasses with grave deliberation and clears his throat. "I'm surprised to find you . . . to find one amongst us who displays signs of cowardice and hides in civilian clothes at the approach of a little danger. How dare you discard the uniform worn by His Majesty's soldiers?" He jerks his hand into a tight salute, as if mere mention of the tsar were enough to call forth feelings of blind loyalty.

"Honestly, Foronov, I. . ."

The upperclassman raises both palms. "Although I regret it deeply, I find myself compelled to report you to your superior officer. Let's go."

"Go where?"

"Don't tell me you're afraid?" With a self-righteous sneer, Foronov draws a revolver with an ivory handle from his pocket.

Fresh blood stains the snow outside. I stare at the blood for a moment before hurrying after Yuri. The Nevsky is deserted except for the men carrying away bodies. We cross the Fontanka, veer right, follow the canal. Distinct bursts of rifle fire float in on gusts of wind. A coal-black cloud of smoke rises to the east. Soon we come alongside a barge. The ice is broken in several places, creating pools of inky water from which vapor rises.

"I'm out of cigarettes," Foronov says. He leads us toward a shop in a one-story brick building, its bright green sign indicating Fresh Colonial Commodities and Other Dainties can be purchased inside. No one answers his knock. "I'll go round back. You two wait here."

On either side of the door are display windows, containing wide-mouthed jars filled with pickled mushrooms and cucumbers. We've come at least a dozen blocks from Dr. Sharin's building. This spur-of-the-moment detour makes me nervous.

"Yuri," I say, my voice firmer now. "Let's get going. My mother..."

"He's a senior. I've got to do what he says."

That's when an olive-green convertible shoots up the street, canvas roof down, siren wailing. I clamp my hands over my ears and implore the Fates to let the car speed past, but it stops a few yards away. I steal a look at the sailor behind the wheel and the soldiers on the running boards. Four others lounge in back with a machine gun. Around their chests hang ammunition clips. Strips of red cloth adorn their lapels. Each man carries a rifle, a revolver tucked into his waistband. Two more men lie on the fenders, bayonets aimed at us.

Pee trickles down my thigh.

"What's the quickest way to the palace bridge?" the driver yells, half rising from his seat. He's tall and square-bodied. Friendly enough. There's a gash on his cheek.

I shake my head, unable to speak.

After a hasty conversation, the men all jump out except for the one with the bloody kerchief tied around his head.

Clasping my arms to my chest to prevent their shaking, I watch him settle behind the wheel.

"Open up, you cursed band of lepers," the sailor hollers and bangs his fist against the shop door.

At a wag of his finger, his companions, who must be deserters, bring their guns crashing down on the display window. Amidst the jangle of broken glass, we hear a muffled cry of protest from within.

Suppressing the wild desire to break into a run, I do my best to attract Yuri's attention: "Psst, psst!"

"Hey, boy."

I go all quiet. It's the man with the bloody kerchief. A paralyzing fear lumps up my throat. I can feel the exact spot on my back between the shoulder blades, where the bullet will lodge. At such close range, I will surely die. Mum will be grief-stricken. Why, oh why, did I tell Yuri I needed that stupid book?

"What do you think of this here revolution?" the man calls.

"I don't know." It's a lie. I know exactly what I think. Mum says we will lose everything if these thugs manage to overthrow the regime. I step away, eyes never leaving the deserter, whose disgruntled expression makes me hasten to add, "I think, I am quite sure, that it's all right."

"Sure is all right," he says with a grunt of pleasure. "Equality, freedom, that's what it is."

My crab-steps have brought me closer to Yuri. "Shouldn't we be on our way?" I manage, a tremor in my voice.

"Hold on." The man fumbles with his lapel and unpins his red ribbon.

"Here, Comrade." He presses his lips together in a grimace of determination. "Take this and wear it, this badge of freedom."

Although my legs feel as wobbly as the meat aspic entrée we were served last night at dinner, I shuffle over to the car and thread the ribbon through a buttonhole on my overcoat. "Thank you very much. Good . . . good luck."

The sailor steps out of the shop examining a piece of paper, no doubt directions to the bridge. He folds the paper into his pocket. Simultaneously, Foronov emerges from behind the building. His face is flushed scarlet.

"What in the heck is that! Where did you pick up that ribbon?"

"Leave him alone," Yuri shout-whispers. "Let's get out of here."

"With you two? Not unless your pal removes the ribbon," Foronov says as the revolutionaries encircle us.

"Why shouldn't he wear a ribbon?" The sailor nudges his companions who all snicker at his sarcastic tone.

Lips pursed with annoyance, Foronov buttons up his chamois gloves. "Make it snappy. Throw that damn thing away."

"Throw it away?" The sailor's eyes have become slits.

"My friend here was only kidding," Yuri says.

"No, wait. Let's hear what he has to say." The sailor cocks his head. "Why not, lieutenant?" A hint of menace has crept into his voice. The golden epaulettes must have made him mistake Foronov for an officer.

Their argument reminds me of a puppet show I attended in Rome the year before Papa died. We sat on wooden benches. Pulcinella clobbered the other puppet, wielding a nightstick.

Mum found it funny, but I kept my eyes shut most of the time, certain the show would not end well.

Foronov barely succeeds in controlling his temper. The color drains from his face as he reels off the military school creed: "Because, a soldier of His Majesty . . ."

"His Majesty indeed! Nicholas the Second? The second and last. What do we care about him? It's Nico . . . Nicolasha," the sailor spits out. "Yeah. Nicolasha, that's all he is to us. His Majesty? That's over. No more such."

"What nerve to speak like that of His Imperial Majesty. Enough!"

"Enough is right," the sailor snarls. "We're the law now. Got that? The law. As for your precious Nicholas the Second, Imperial Majesty, and all that crap, that's what we fought and defeated. It's Nicolasha to us, plain nothing." He fixes on Foronov a look of intense hatred. "Remove those initials immediately."

The sailor flings out an arm and tears off one of the epaulettes. He spits on it, tosses it to the ground.

Foronov whips out his revolver and shoots.

Yuri and I exchange glances, dumbfounded.

What an idiot! Don't they teach diplomacy at his stupid military school?

In two seconds flat the soldiers have disarmed the upperclassman. They grab his shoulders, move toward the canal, swing his body over the railing. He falls onto the ice, which cracks open.

"Help!" he cries, clutching the rim of the hole.

The soldier with the gash on his cheek raises his rifle, aims, and fires. Foronov's body slips below the murky water. The ripples soon vanish. Alone his cap remains afloat.

I can't believe I've witnessed the death of two more people. My throat swells up. I feel sick to my stomach.

The wounded soldier retrieves the folded paper from the sailor's pocket. Once his companions have hoisted the dead body into the backseat, their car speeds away.

We jog through the streets, past the crumbled ruin of the courthouse. Columns of smoke rise into the air. Tears blur my vision. My cousin's face is ashen. I know what I want to say—*Told you so. We should have paid more attention to your valet—*but what good would it do to lord this over him now?

A bit farther on, we are startled to find ourselves behind a barricade: piled carts, wooden crates, discarded furniture. Suspended from a rifle wedged into a wicker basket, a piece of red cloth confirms my fear that life has taken a new direction.

We hurry along in silence. At the river, we follow the deserted quay. The daylight turns soft, and the sun sinks below the horizon. Purple tints the snow. Yuri fishes a key from his pocket. That's when I realize I left *813* on Dr. Sharin's windowsill. I won't tell Mum. She's upset enough as is. I'll let her know after all this is over, after our return from Southern Russia. We'll laugh about it then, once home and back to life as normal.

The Picnic

I passed the examination, even answered the tougher questions, like the one about the implications of Kutuzov's decision to abandon Moscow. I managed to write several pages and left school feeling satisfied with myself. To celebrate, Mum bought me chocolate, Elena prepared a picnic, and I invited Sergei Tolstoy to spend the afternoon at the beach. He's fifteen and I was beginning to fear he might not show up, but here he comes now, whistling a merry tune. Tolstoy carries what appears to be a parasol. He glances behind him, scans the dacha windows for onlookers, and shoves the parasol into the bushes.

"My mother insisted," he says with a shrug.

I smile, pleased that we have more in common than simply being schoolmates. Tolstoy's blond hair has been cut short. Mine is down to my shoulders since Mum has *more important things* on her mind these days. I have started wearing it in a ponytail.

The sea is so blue today. Perfect weather.

We admire the view from the edge of the cliff before descending the wobbly old staircase. Puffs of white clouds float on the horizon. My pocket is full of superb round flat stones, saved for just such an occasion.

"You come here often?" I ask.

"Every summer. Where do you go?"

"Khotelovo."

"Where's that?"

"Estonia. Near Pskov?"

"Bet you don't have a beach as nice as this one."

It's my turn to shrug. No argument there. I stare out at the Black Sea.

We reach the bottom steps and jump into the sand. Tolstoy sheds his shoes and socks and races into the water. I pull off my shirt and join him. We splash about for a while. Tolstoy spreads out his towel on the shore so we can sit down. I've brought the picnic Elena prepared.

"Hey, this is good," he says, biting into a cold meat patty. "Did your cook come with you?"

"Elena makes them. She was our lady's maid."

"Well, she sure knows how to make pirozhki."

"My mother is going to sell pirozhki," I tell him, not sure how this information will be received. "She's starting a business."

"No kidding?"

To my relief, there's no contempt in his voice. Only surprise.

"Nobody knows how to cook and the restaurants in Odessa have become so expensive that she decided to sell meals, since Elena's a good cook."

I do not say that first Mum tried peddling cigarettes at Arcadia, the main beach downtown. She told us she gave it up because of varicose veins, but I think the idea of chance encounters with acquaintances from Petersburg proved too demoralizing. I'm glad she has come up with this new catering scheme.

The sand feels silky beneath my feet. I hand Tolstoy the last *pirozhok* and fish my stones out of my pocket.

"It was scary last week when the Red Guards were here. Did they come to your house too, Serezha?"

Tolstoy nods. "Sure did. But that's nothing compared to the Cheka."

"What's the Cheka?"

"They wear leather jackets. They're hoodlums Papa says, but now they've signed up as secret police, which is a disaster since they have power and commit dreadful deeds." He closes his eyes tight and grimaces, so dreadful are the deeds committed by the Cheka.

"Like what?"

"Skin people?"

"Ugh!" I peer over at him lest he's pulling my leg, but no. Tolstoy is serious.

"There's this one guy downtown. Johnson. He's got a black soul. He does kill the people though, after skinning them."

I want to find out how he knows such things but do not dare to ask. Nobody in my family would ever tell me anything like this, not even Elena. "People must hate Johnson," I say cautiously, in the hope he'll say more.

"Fear him is more likely. Here in Odessa, the Cheka kills around fifty people a day."

"But, why?"

"No reason. People like you and me. That's why we're leaving."

My heart skips a beat. "Leaving?"

"Thinking of leaving," he corrects himself. "Aren't you?"

I mutter an affirmative response but should have said no. Yesterday I overheard my aunt declare that she refuses to abandon her country. She was adamant about it. Elena is too old to travel abroad. As for Mum, I know her well enough to realize she won't agree to leave Russia until my brother has been located.

War, revolution, execution. I must now add Cheka to my list of horrible things. I let Tolstoy skip all my stones. My heart just isn't in it anymore.

Out of This World

I never meant to abandon my children. How could anyone think me capable of such deceit? It should go without saying that I wanted to raise Valeria and Nadine myself. Desertion? Who deserts children on purpose? Such an attentive mother I tried to be, during their infancy anyway. It pains me to recognize the level of misunderstanding my departure provoked. Oh, the finger pointing, the acrimonious comments! I can still hear the vicious voices in Paris all those years ago. *What kind of woman would behave that way? How self-centered. How cruel.* The truth is I intended to return. Give it a good year was my plan. I had everything figured out, month by month. But the trip to California turned out to be such a challenge ...

The idea of being in pictures hit when I was five, way before leaving Russia. I remember the day the governess told my mother what a fine little actress I would grow up to be. Summer 1908, if I'm not mistaken. I took what Mademoiselle Lorient said to heart. And then there was my hair. Mama's friends would slither fingers through the silky stuff trying to capture its magnificence. So many strangers admired what grew on my head that I started to believe I was truly special. Red-gold hair like mine bestowed superiority. First in Moscow, later in Constantinople and Paris, I would stand in front of the mirror with that Hollywood starlet look in the eye. Titian blond hair, like the golden-haired beauties of medieval Italy, that's what my head grew all my life. So, blame the hair. Blame the

Bolshevik Revolution. Blame my inability to pass the bacca-laureate exam. But don't blame me.

Fortunately, my lovelies inherited brown hair from their father. That was about all he left them before his suicide. It was a relief to know they wouldn't judge themselves superior or be led astray.

But I'm digressing. Where was I? Ah, yes. My journey to the United States in 1924. First, the train to Normandy and that wretched tramp steamer from Cherbourg on rough seas, then a bus from New York City, straight across the country. I rode a Pickwick night coach into Los Angeles. My heart skipped a beat as the driver passed all those orange trees. I still love orange trees, although I can no longer smell the orange blossoms.

Was I ever a wreck upon arrival. Dirty, dusty, tired, hungry. When the bus pulled up in front of the Union Stage Depot, I didn't hesitate. I treated myself to a taxicab. I had the address of a rooming house, The Rookery. I felt right at home because a couple from Kyiv lived down the hall. We spoke Russian together. Zinaida took me under her wing. I stayed a couple of months, enough time to get my bearings. A girl always needs to get her bearings. What pleasant walks we shared. I loved the lush vegetation and the palm trees and the bird of para-dise outside my window. Sometimes we rode the streetcar to Venice Beach. The route crossed Culver City, which wasn't developed yet. We passed bean fields and walnut orchards.

Culver City remains one of my favorite haunts with its film studios, especially now that one of my great-grandsons is a resident. Paul designs movie sets for Universal. His daugh-ter Juliet has a turned-up nose like me and red-gold hair.

The darling girl spends hours at the computer, playing a game called Minecraft. She has a habit of talking to herself and describes each click of the mouse. Whenever I visit, I hover behind her and listen. "The sun is starting to set. Oh, yeah. I forgot. There! A door for the garden. Ready to play. Better hurry 'cuz it's sunset soon. The Endermen and spiders come out at night. Uh-oh. We might get attacked. But I have safety. I can fly."

My girls would have loved Minecraft had computers existed when they were young. Mama looked after them in our apartment on the Rue de Monttessuy. My sister Olga helped with homework. I did my best to make amends. I attended all their birthday parties, accompanied them to dance lessons and art school. I offered encouragement while they copied poems into their *cahiers de poésie*, listened as they recited La Fontaine. While they went about their lives, I chattered away, doing my utmost to clear up what had grown into a major kerfuffle. Suffice it to say they paid me no heed. The only one who recognized me was the cat. As soon as I slipped into the room, Koshka would prick up his ears and start hissing, back arched, claws extended.

Valeria lives on in that same apartment building. There's a superb view of the Eiffel Tower from the balcony. The deli across the street has belonged to an Arab since the nineties. As for Nadine, she raised three children in Ville d'Avray and married a doctor, Michel Chekhov. Yes, *those* Chekhovs. He died several years ago but I haven't run into him.

I continue to divide my time between France and the United States. Oh, how I do love to fly. Over hills and dales I speed, zinging this way and that.

I must admit to having developed a commercial-aviation habit of late. For long journeys, I let myself indulge. I'll hop a plane at LAX. No reservations required. I like the fact that should the plane crash, I won't be among the victims. With the cool air currents, the passengers don't notice as I weave my way up and down the aisles. If I encounter any obnoxious kids, I float to the rear, where the stewardesses sit in case of turbulence.

Weightlessness is delicious. Once in a while I try to explain to my lovelies what they can look forward to. This altered state is like staying young forever. My sister Olga gets it. She's ninety-nine and has lived in California since the French left Morocco and the government appropriated her fruit business. What a dreadful time that was. But wait. Before we proceed, let's dispel some misconceptions.

1. Ghosts are not evil, and we don't rattle chains.
2. News flash on cemeteries: Ghosts don't stay underground or lurk behind tombstones in the hopes of scaring passersby.
3. It doesn't hurt to go through walls.
4. The white light is a one-way phenomenon. Think of passing over as a celestial "meet and greet." But dipping back down, yes. We can do that whenever we please.
5. Reincarnation does exist but it's not obligatory. Free choice is the rule. That's what the Afterlife is all about.

So, I choose to dip back in, as I was explaining, my most recent trip being to California, Riverside to be precise. Olga claims to have chosen Southern California in order to research my disappearance, but that's a fib if you ask me. In my opinion, she came for the weather. How do I know? She gave up the search as soon as the authorities told her it was absurd to try and locate someone who had gone missing in downtown LA over thirty years ago.

Olga lived in five different countries before moving to the United States: Russia, Turkey, France, Germany, Morocco. For years, I trailed her around and tried my best to leave clues. Unfortunately, she never noticed the feathers I blew in her path or the doors I pushed open. It goes without saying that I kept close tabs on my sister, especially in Berlin during the war. Bombs exploded outside as she lay in a hospital bed, giving birth. I kept repeating that Reiner was a cad, that he had another mistress, but my efforts were all in vain. After the Paris Peace Treaties of 1947, she decided to raise her son in Morocco, what with the sunshine.

I'm glad to report Olga was able to hear me once she celebrated her ninety-ninth birthday. We've been having great conversations. It worries her son Ilya who called the hospice team to say she has been having "hallucinations." Hah!

I told her the whole story a few months ago. How Zinaida clued me in that they were casting dancers for the prologue at Grauman's Egyptian Theater. I auditioned and had to show up for work the next day. The pay was only thirty-five bucks a week, but I went out and rented a proper one-bedroom at The Terraces, near the Garden Court Apartments on Hollywood Boulevard. That was about the time I met Myrna Loy. We became good friends that spring. How we laughed at the skimpy costumes they made us wear, burlap tunics with slits on the side, cut in such a way that the tunics kept slipping off our skinny shoulders. We were both hired for *The Ten*

Commandments. Twice a day we did our dance routines. There was an orchestra and at least 100 dancers on stage. What fun it was to perform in front of a live audience. For dinner, we'd go across the street to Musso & Frank Grill. I liked their Caesar salad. The eggs were coddled, not hard-boiled. Naturally, I never splurged, saving money to wire home to Paris.

It was Myrna who got the big break and the rest is history. She was a redhead, like me. Beautiful auburn hair. (Just for the record, auburn is darker and Titian blond has more gold. Whatever the shade, people focused on the two of us in that chorus line.)

Sensing success around the corner, I hired a manager. Herbie gave me expensive earrings, inspired by the discovery of King Tut's tomb. He was extremely enthusiastic about my career options. "You're absolutely gorgeous, out of this world, the cat's meow." He said I'd be following in Myrna's footsteps in no time. We went on a couple dates before I concluded that it would be better not to mix social life with business. Herbie did get me auditions though and a role in a silent film. Zinaida introduced us. Oh, I know. I should have checked his references more thoroughly. My sister claims that was my first mistake.

These days Olga and I watch a lot of soap operas together. There's a show I like. It's on once a week, Saturday nights: *Celebrity Ghost Stories.* She lives on Chestnut Street, in a yellow Victorian, haunted by some former residents which means I have to hustle to secure the ceiling corner, the best view of her television set by far. Imagine my surprise when the host began to describe what happened to a certain starlet with strawberry blond hair, back in the twenties. I paid close attention because he said the episode had been filmed on Hollywood Boulevard where I rented that one-bedroom. The actress explains that her intention to date other men sent her manager into a jealous rage. The camera pans to a claw-foot tub and he's pushing her body underwater while she gasps for air. I flew down and perched over Olga's shoulder.

"No!" I screamed. "That's not right. He murdered me with a serrated kitchen knife. Your script makes no sense. Why would I haunt that grungy old building? It's the last place on earth I'd want to be."

As I lay there dying, I prayed no one would ever hurt my girls. Nadine has eight great grandchildren now, and Valeria devoted all her energy to the London branch of Save the Children until her retirement in 1990. Although I watched over them the best I could, my inability to communicate meant I was never able to apologize for my absence, a fact I sincerely regret. The good news is my prayers have been answered. They have both lived long happy lives. I guess everything works out in the end.

Walnuts

She seems to like me and is nice enough, although rather plump,
Kolia thought, peering past her toward the Pacific Ocean, past
the gazebo and formal garden where her white poodle had
run, leaping from the terrace to chase a butterfly across the
yard, large by Santa Monica standards, a yard that belonged,
of course, to her parents who owned the pharmaceutical firm
that had allowed them to purchase this mansion, she had said
at the beginning of the luncheon, not without embarrassment,
when he asked a simple question, not meant to aggravate but
more for something to say while the butler poured a glass of
Sauterne and served the second course, chicken and mushroom casserole dotted with slivers of white truffle imported
from France, a dish he could have eaten at his parents' table
before the revolution but now seemed an extravagance, considering that only last week he had trekked all the way from
Hollywood to West Adams Boulevard in order to gather wal-
nuts and avoid starvation, an act of desperation he felt ashamed
to admit, even in a joking manner, to this woman who had
been so impressed by his background and title, meaningless
outside Russia, and who hoped to become his wife. It was only
after her dog returned and she placed a piece of chicken breast
in its mouth with her fingers that he understood the difference
in their circumstances was insurmountable and decided not
to see her again.

The Announcement

Irina was seated on the velvet sofa, knees drawn up to cushion a heavy reference book. By night, the sofa doubled as her bed. She groaned when her father called her into the kitchen. Pavel Pavlovich had come home early. With reluctance, she joined her mother at the aluminum-legged table. Even by French standards, their kitchen was tiny. She reached out and removed a dead leaf from the pot of African violets. Outside, rain fell on the cemetery that served as a view.

Irina drummed her fingers on the table. She hoped to finish a reading assignment and spend the afternoon with a friend whose father had promised two passes to the *Foire de Paris* at the Porte de Versailles. France was a wonderful country with free education in high schools and technical schools and secretarial schools that guaranteed advancement in life. If she studied hard enough, obtaining a degree from the Sorbonne might be a possibility. She picked up *Poslednie Novosti* and glanced at the date. May 19, 1929. Three weeks until her first baccalaureate exam.

Her father did not sit down. He swept a few breadcrumbs from lunch into a circle on the blue Formica tabletop, pushing in at the edges with his fingertips. His striped jacket appeared more faded than usual. Pavel Pavlovich had owned the jacket since Constantinople, where the cabaret manager required identical outfits of all bartenders and busboys. When he began to speak in Russian, his voice shook with emotion. "I have something to say. Please listen."

Alexandra Petrovna was knitting him a pullover with raglan sleeves from gray wool purchased on sale at the Samaritaine. Her needles clicked as she worked.

Irina arranged herself to more closely resemble the obedient daughter her parents expected her to be. Pavel Pavlovich cleared his throat and sighed, his eyes circling the ceiling. He had returned home that afternoon with a bottle of artisanal vodka, an unnecessary expense in her opinion. It was impossible to keep track of his movements now that he had burdened himself with two jobs.

"I have. . ." He paused before settling on a ponderous tone for what he intended to say. "Over the years, you've both heard me speak of my desire to emigrate."

"Excuse me. We *did* emigrate. We left our homeland to live with frogs. Frogs, frogs, frogs. France is a country of frogs."

Irina pulled a long face. "Please don't say such things, Maman."

Pavel Pavlovich took out a handkerchief and wiped his brow. "Lapushka, give me a chance to explain, would you?"

"No need," Alexandra Petrovna replied. "We came here as stateless refugees. Several years ago, we applied for Nansen passports. The plan was to hold on to them until the Soviet experiment failed. As soon as that happened, we were supposed to return to our homeland." She nodded in agreement with herself as if there were no room for doubt and placed her knitting on the table so she could devote herself entirely to the defense of her opinion. "That's what you said."

"I didn't."

"Oh, yes, you did."

"We've had this discussion before." Pavel Pavlovich gave another sigh, less resigned this time. "And that's not what I wanted to talk about."

"Oh? And what did you want to talk about?"

"Emigration. You both met my friend Sergei Tolstoy who drives the taxi. His older brother and I attended law school together. Sergei went to the American Embassy last week for information on visas. Moving to the United States has always been a dream of mine. To see New York with its skyscrapers and–"

"No money." Alexandra Petrovna cut him off. The cadence of her voice made their pecuniary troubles sound permanent.

"Amen to that." Apollon said, giving in to pure irritation. "And why don't we have the money? Let me tell you why. We don't have the money because you buried those brooches in Odessa."

Alexandra Petrovna didn't seem to be listening. "Farewell totally impractical dream." She slapped her palms together like a baker after popping a cake into the oven. "That puts an end to that."

"Actually, it doesn't."

Irina raised her eyes. She had been reading a brochure that promised tips on how to pass the baccalaureate. Her parents were bickering. This wasn't new. She tuned in to what had been said and uttered a little noise, a sharp inhalation at realizing the significance of their argument.

"Here's my plan. I'll take a steamer to America. Once established in a job, probably in New York City, I'll send for you both."

It was Irina who interrupted this time. "Papa, I don't think I want to go to America. I'm working hard at being French." She bit back sudden tears. "My friends would miss me if I left Paris. And I'd miss them."

"Speak Russian!" Alexandra Petrovna hissed and retrieved her knitting.

Pavel Pavlovich's face had assumed a pained expression. He sat down at the table and lined up two shot glasses. With a shrug of acceptance, he uncorked the vodka bottle. "This morning I booked passage one-way. I'm leaving in two weeks with Sergei and his brother. From Cherbourg."

His words hung in the air. Irina knew he had put a full stop at the end of his existence in Russia and yearned for new horizons, but she had not expected him to set the ball rolling. And he wasn't asking permission. His mind was made up.

Alexandra Petrovna gasped. "How are we going to live?" She worked her fingers along the knitting needle, acting like the stitches had become beads on a rosary. "How will we survive?"

"You'll need to move. I'll wire money."

"We won't be able to afford this flat."

"I've located a rooming house in Bois-Colombes. Rue de Chatou. The next town over. Not much will change. Same train to Paris. Same shops. Same markets. The owner welcomes tenants of Russian ancestry. You can stay there until I've earned enough to bring you both to America."

He placed a glass of vodka in front of his wife. She pushed herself away from the table. "Not me. I'm not celebrating. Celebrate by yourself."

Irina clapped a hand to her forehead. "I can't believe it. You're leaving us? Oh, Papa. Say it's not so."

Pavel Pavlovich lifted his glass. "Here's to our future. May it be . . . all we want it to be."

Irina leapt to her feet. She snatched up a sweater and her raincoat and left the flat, slamming the door behind her.

No Imposition

Volodia stands in a corridor at Maison Russe, clasping a bouquet of yellow roses that are already past their prime. A heavyset woman dressed in a nurse's uniform passes with a bedpan. Russian voices can be heard on the stairs. He pauses at a bulletin board marked Ville de Saint-Geneviève-des-Bois, 1932, and reads the list of activities: bridge, art class, stamp collecting. More paint has chipped off the woodwork since his last visit. Slowly he climbs to the first floor and enters a high-ceilinged private room. A woman with gray hair loose around her shoulders is seated in a pale blue armchair beside a south-facing window. To the right, there's an improvised altar with icons and squat red candles. Only one is lit.

"You're looking well, Mamochka," he says, before swinging around to arrange the roses in a vase. His eyes find the photo of his brother in uniform, the tsar's initials embroidered on the golden epaulettes. Nika's photo is the only other object on the dresser. His mother hasn't framed any of the proofs Lisa must have provided. "Is that a new . . . nightgown?"

Marie Nikolaievna strokes the fabric, a faraway look in her eye.

"It is. You just missed your aunt. She says hello."

"Does she? What's it like, living with her again?" He pulls up a Louis XVI chair, the design of its upholstery alternating columns of beige and faded crimson. "Not as bad as you anticipated?"

Marie Nikolaievna turns her head to stare out the window. "Hot today, isn't it?"

The weather was not what he wanted to talk about. He frowned. "They forecast record highs. All week long, in fact."

"Good. I prefer hot weather."

"I've brought you something from the Russian artists' exhibit at the Salle Gaveau." Volodia places a brochure in his mother's lap. "You should go. It would do you good."

"What is that supposed to mean?"

His aim was to be jovial. So far, he had not succeeded.

"You need to get out. See people."

"I do see people. Plenty of people."

"Where?"

"At meals."

"You should come into the city more often."

"I'd have to pay for food and transportation. Nothing draws me to Paris. There's no one I particularly care to see. You and Lisa come here, albeit less frequently than before."

"We could meet at the Gare d'Orsay. If it's a matter of money . . ." His voice trails off.

"I told you. I'm trying to avoid expense. I just paid for shoes."

Volodia takes a shoebox from the side table and opens it. "Wedge shoes? Nice."

"For the garden. I like to sit and listen to birdsong. The air is fragrant. It's almost paradise out there under the linden trees."

There's a silence. Volodia shifts in his seat. "Oak, I think, Mum."

"Oak then."

"I brought you roses. Yellow, like at Khotelovo."

"Khotelovo . . . Oksana Semenovna made such beautiful bouquets. Remember how she wrote me about having cried when they led our cows away?"

"How's darling Lisa?"

"She'll be coming home from Corsica soon. At least she's been able to act like a human being for two weeks and not a doll."

"It was good to see her at Easter."

"You should get together more often."

"I know what you think. No need to repeat it."

"She sent two letters and a telegram from Calvi. And this." Marie Nikolaievna brings her hand to her breast and kneads the fabric between her thumb and index finger. "So soft."

"Is that why you didn't get dressed? I was afraid you had been depressed again."

"It's not depression."

"Melancholy?"

"Melancholy, yes. I don't want to do anything. It must be nostalgia for our country, for what we have lost. For our lifestyle. Nostalgia for our estates and town houses. I feel like I left part of myself behind in Russia. Don't you feel that way too?"

"Not really. I guess it's easier for my generation."

"But look at you! About to turn 29, and how do you spend your time?"

"My life is full."

"And Lisa. Your sister divorced her poor husband. She accepts invitations from married Frenchmen."

"This is France, Mum. Remember?"

"She hasn't put any money aside and soon she'll be too old to model. What will she do then? Count on the goodwill of others? Who will pay her rent? Buy her pretty things?"

"She doesn't have to live in the sixteenth arrondissement. It's a choice."

"As a mother, I did not expect this destiny for you both."

"No one holds you responsible."

"No grandchildren either."

"Maman!"

"The revolution tore apart our lives and the lives of so many other decent men and women. You throw a pebble into a stream, and it creates ripples for a while. The ripples end and the surface of the water stills. With a revolution, the ripples go on forever."

"I think I have assimilated quite well. I have an apartment in Boulogne. Bread on the table."

"Man is not nourished by bread alone. The heart aspires to greater heights."

"I like my job. Being a civil servant suits me." A scream collects in his chest and an inexplicable desire to extricate himself from the situation overwhelms him. "I should go."

"Volodia?"

"Yes, Mum."

"You're good to come see me. I hope it isn't too much of an imposition. You do know what day it is?"

"I do."

"Fourteen years ago, Nika left me."

"May his soul rest in peace."

Volodia lets the scowl fall away from his face, reminding himself of the purpose of this visit. Long ago he promised his mother that she would never be alone on Nika's death day. He bends to kiss her forehead.

"Let's say a prayer. Help me up, sweetheart. Would you?"

The Horror of It All

Kira and Aleksei Shvetzov were supposed to take their new baby to meet Aleksei's parents on the Champs Elysées but, after breakfast, Kira announced she wanted to stay home. Aleksei, who sat hunched on the sofa shuffling the Sunday morning papers, didn't acknowledge this statement. Instead, he held out the front page of Le Figaro, which showed the S. S. Normandie, off on its maiden voyage.

"Imagine," he said, cigarette bobbing at his lip. "She'll dock in New York by the middle of next week."

Aleksei was a stocky man with protuberant eyes and a stiffness of manner that discouraged all argument. Kira shushed him with an eyeroll toward the darkened entryway, encumbered by Misha's carriage and several boxes of art supplies. As she reclaimed their pack of Camels, her fierce blue eyes darted around their studio, located on a side street in Courbevoie. After all that had happened, she couldn't help but wish they were on that ocean liner, invigorated by the salty air, off for North America, where her mother and sister had resided ever since the Bolshevik Revolution made them refugees. From New York, they'd catch a train to Toronto.

She cranked open the balcony door, stepped outside, and lit her first Camel of the day, hoping the nicotine would calm her nerves. Kira had been fourteen when she left Moscow. Life as an immigrant had not been easy, especially after her father's suicide. She had learned to create artificial flowers for a workers' co-op at seventeen, an opportunity that had led to regular work but meant giving up all dreams of art school. Her wages now helped stretch the meager salary Aleksei earned from his perfume industry job. He maintained they needed a bigger apartment. What they needed was a fresh start.

On the street below, a florist was setting out buckets of flowers. The scent of peonies made it possible to forget the stink of the city, the studio they could barely afford, and Aleksei's intransigence on matters related to family. His lack of empathy bothered her more than their cramped quarters. It was Kira who had proposed, fearful of becoming an old maid. At times, she felt an emotion close to remorse at having taken initiative, especially once his original ardor cooled. Perhaps the difference in age—he was five years younger—explained their relationship difficulties.

"Yes, I'll stay home," she repeated, unwilling to let the subject drop. "Go alone. And when you get back, let's talk more about moving to Canada."

"Talk more? I think not. It would kill Mama were I to leave France."

She waited to see whether he would elaborate. He cracked his knuckles, locked his hands behind his head. They exchanged glances.

The first notes of Damia's jazzy rendition of "Night and Day" floated skyward. The half-deaf florist, a Great War veteran, played his radio at full blast. Kira placed a hand on her belly and stepped back inside. Her presence wasn't required to show off Misha. At four months, their son accepted puréed food as well as breast milk. The thought made her perk up.

Aleksei, who had returned to his newspaper, shot her a final sideways glance as she headed into the bathroom.

She took one last drag on her cigarette and stubbed it out in the sink, twisting long after the fire had died. There were things her husband needed to know. Not once had he questioned why she avoided her in-laws. When they dropped by six months ago, she had stayed in Paris all afternoon, claiming a last-minute career opportunity—the creation of a flowered hatband commissioned by one of Matisse's favorite models.

She leaned toward the mirror and drew a careful crimson line around the contours of her mouth. Wearing her wavy brown hair pulled back into an array of curls at the neckline did nothing to improve her looks. Lipstick helped.

She crossed the room and flopped herself down at the worktable. Her fingers caressed the mauve silk, already cut into petals. She'd devote the afternoon to silk flowers, an income-producing activity neglected since Misha's birth, an activity that helped her relax, not at all tedious, as some Russian émigrés claimed. The flowers were easy to assemble once the petals had been dipped in gelatin and hung up to dry.

"They'll be disappointed not to see you," Aleksei said, unhooking one arm of his wire spectacles to wipe a bit of lint or maybe a tear from his left eye. His hair was slicked back from his forehead with pomade. "Let me ring them up. Perhaps we can meet at that tearoom you like. It's within walking distance."

"Say I'm ill," Kira snapped.

She could guess what Aleksei was thinking. He maintained her mood swings during pregnancy should have ended. Sure enough, that's exactly what he said. He went on and on about how offended his mother would be, using words like *inappropriate* and *intolerable* and *outrageous*, although he wasn't close to his parents who lavished their attention on an elder sibling and her three children. The seven of them lived together in Bougival, near Versailles. Kira shuddered at the thought of her fateful visit to their cottage: the pungent odor of fresh paint, black to match the drapery, the bamboo wind chimes Aleksei's aunt had sent from Harbin, China, tinkling a warning from the front yard, the bust of Julius Caesar crashing to the floor.

Her husband was a stickler for appearances, the result of a strict upbringing as the stepson of a former White Army officer. On the mantelpiece he kept a family photo taken several years after arrival in France. She picked up the photo and scanned faces. Aleksei in childhood, hair slicked back, suit too tight, flanked by his elegant mother Victoria Alexievna and the Colonel, a supercilious grin on his face. Poor Aleksei, only five when his own father died, stoned to death by Bolshevik sympathizers. To make matters worse, Victoria Alexievna had given her children the Colonel's surname. Kira slipped the silver frame into a drawer. Head to one side, Aleksei cast his eyes upward. She prepared herself to respond to his protest but all he did was snatch the pack of Camels out of her hand. His eyelid twitched as he drew smoke deep into his lungs.

Squinting against the smoke, she took a deep breath and said in a rush, "Last year the Colonel made advances. You were in Toulouse." She spoke without emotion, having gone over the confession so many times in her head that its delivery conveyed no hint of her own impropriety.

Aleksei pounded the worktable with such force that his fist jostled the tools of her trade, the molds and crochet hooks and bobbins of silk thread all in a row. Closing his eyes for a surprisingly long moment, he soon regained his composure and apologized for the behavior of his stepfather, a man who made light of his reputation as a philanderer, despite rumors of numerous affairs.

This reaction gave her the courage to continue.

"He cornered me in the pantry. Remember when I told you about knocking that ugly old bust off its pedestal? I vowed never to set foot in your parents' house again."

She scrutinized her husband's face to judge whether he understood the implications. Apparently not. His mind seemed to be rehearsing what he intended to tell his mother. His adherence to protocol clashed with the artistic tendencies of the perfume industry folk, at least those who attended their church, a fact that made her wonder how long he could keep his job and reinforced her conviction that they should emigrate. Once settled in North America, she would start her own business, crafting silk flowers for the nascent garment industry there.

Kira swallowed the bile in her throat, all too aware that whatever more she divulged would probably be altered, sanitized, misconstrued. Her husband considered his stepfather as family. The Colonel remained above reproach.

Aleksei squeezed past the carriage and tiptoed across the squeaky parquet toward the telephone, shoulders bowed. With the entryway door open, she overheard every word: the usual niceties, his proposal of the tearoom as an alternative, the short statement about postpartum confinement and her need for bed rest. Aleksei was doing what she had asked. He always did what she asked. No surprise, no whimsy, complete predictability.

Misha whimpered, causing her milk to rise. She tucked the blanket around their son and jiggled the carriage. He was a handsome baby with his full lips and fuzzy blond hair. How fortunate sweet Misha resembled Aleksei, a fact no one could deny.

Kira felt an obligation to say more, so after Aleksei hung up the telephone, she forced herself to return to the day he had left for the violet harvest in Toulouse, jauntily swinging their striped suitcase, his guileless face shiny at the prospect of new responsibilities. It had all begun innocently enough. Colonel Shvetzov had driven them into Paris, affable and charming as ever. Aleksei's stepfather had found employment early on as a chauffeur. He worked for a prominent French couturier whose career required periodic trips to Milan. Members of the White Russian community in Paris considered the car a perk of the job. He did keep the Delahaye in perfect condition. Glossy exterior, spotless chassis, gleaming rosewood dashboard. His diligence was undeniable.

They had risen early for a Saturday. After Aleksei disappeared into the train station, the colonel maneuvered his way over the cobblestones and back through the city. They passed the Avenue des Gobelins, the Rue de la Glacière, the Rue du Faubourg Saint-Jacques. How remarkable it felt to ride in that sleek car with its spiffy white-wall tires. A passenger in a vehicle like that could easily pretend the revolution had never occurred. Kira removed her cloche because its hawk feather tickled the skin on her neck. While the car was stopped at a traffic light, the colonel suggested a walk through the Luxembourg Garden. He reached across her knees, barely touching them, opened the glove compartment, took out a pack of cigarettes, lit two Chesterfields.

"A woman like you will be bored without your husband. Why not come out to Bougival for a spell?"

"I wouldn't want to be of any trouble," she said, accepting the smoke.

"Oh, but I insist."

And that was that.

Kira assumed that they would spend the day with Aleksei's mother and sister. A former servant had followed the Shvetsovs abroad and was renowned for her pirozhki, stuffed with minced meat and onions. Who could decline a home-cooked meal and a stroll along the Seine, their regular weekend activity? La Grenouillère wouldn't be open, but she derived pleasure from simply walking the riverbank where a generation of artists had found inspiration. She liked to form an image in her mind of Monet, Renoir, Sisley, and Pissarro setting off to paint, an easel under one arm.

In Bougival, the car slowed to a crawl and crunched its way across the pebbles in the circular driveway. It was at that moment that the colonel swiveled his gaze as if she were precious cargo, a prize no man was good enough to deserve. With a gallant gesture, he opened the car door and escorted her into the quiet house.

"Where is everyone?" she asked with astonishment.

"Ina is off today. Masha took the children to a puppet show. Aleksei's mother is at a charity event, organized by the ladies of the Alexander Nevsky Cathedral."

"But we'll be alone."

"Until lunchtime. And I relish the opportunity to know you better."

After they had removed their coats, the colonel opened a bottle of champagne. He complimented her on her complexion and well-turned ankles. Flattered by the attention, Kira played along until he thrust himself against her in the pantry. The memory produced a shiver of excitement. It was at such times that she felt truly alive, despite the horror of it all.

Kira gnawed her lower lip and drew a handkerchief from her sleeve, reluctant to reveal the full extent of her mischief. She had flirted but so little. Aleksei deserved better if they were to continue as man and wife. Tucking a renegade curl back into place, she leaned her slender body against the wall, beside the framed poster he had carried back from London after their honeymoon. Her eyes scanned the familiar caption: *Cockfosters Station opens 31st July into new country by Underground through trains from Piccadilly.* What might he do? Break her neck? Throw her from the balcony? She had struggled for so long to keep the rape a secret, comforting herself with the probability that Aleksei had sired their child.

The phone call ended. He replaced the receiver in its cradle. Misha started to cry.

Kira dropped her eyes to her fingers, stained yellow by cigarettes. "Pay attention," she said, her voice shrill, knotting and unknotting the handkerchief. "You're missing the point. He forced himself on me while you were away."

Aleksei opened his eyes wide. His expression slowly shifted to one of shame. "Hey, come here, you," he said in a gruff whisper and pulled her toward him. "How I wish Mama had never remarried. I'm so sorry. Please accept my apology."

Kira felt the warmth of his hand on her back. Her hot tears fell more profusely on her cowl-neck blouse, wet with milk from her swollen breasts. She had figured on reproach, insult, denial, not sympathy.

"People say life is easier in Canada. Let's go to Toronto. Take a ship from Southampton."

"Mama will object."

He said these words without conviction, encouraging her to forge ahead. "What about me and Misha? Aren't we your family now?"

Kira felt a surge of hope that their marriage could be saved. Once in Toronto, Aleksei could file a petition and reclaim his real surname: Gorchakov. They'd be able to start over and forget the past. Misha would grow up Canadian. He'd have a nationality, a country, a real passport. Without delay, she packed their suitcase, which smelled faintly of the sugared violets Aleksei had purchased at the Marché aux Violettes des Jacobins in Toulouse and forgotten, tucked deep inside an interior pocket.

Time of the
Pale Green Light

———————

1.

Shanghai was all Marie-Paule had hoped it would be and more, so when Alastair barged in to warn her about a supposed Japanese invasion, interrupting a violin lesson with her star pupil Henry Townley, she shook her head and gently pushed her suitor back out the door. "No means no, Alastair darling," she said. "I won't go."

It was a hot day at the beginning of August 1937. Muggy, with no breeze whatsoever.

Marie-Paule had already refused his proposal of marriage, twice in fact: once at the Opera House, where his chauffeur had driven them to hear the Cossack Chorus, and a second time at the Jessfield Park teahouse, three months later. She shut her eyes and fingered her pearls. Alastair E. Jones was overweight, with puffy red cheeks and prematurely white hair, a man who sweated more than she would have thought possible. He wore single-breasted suits of cream-colored linen and a gardenia boutonnière. His job representing Courvoisier in the Far East meant free samples, and this visit was no exception: an unopened bottle sat in her Cognac cannon, ready for replacement with the empty.

Behind them, Henry knelt beside her wicker plant stand, filled with potted orchids, and snapped his violin case closed.

Marie-Paule straightened the cage of her mynah bird, a present from a former pupil whose family had relocated to London.

"Oh, my goodness!" the bird squawked, darting back and forth on its perch.

"You must pack essentials and accompany me to the docks," Alastair stammered.

"I think Mr. Jones could do with some distraction," she whispered to Henry, willing him into the role of co-conspirator. "Demonstrate your flexibility exercise. Would you please?"

The eight-year-old thrust his hand deep into a pocket and withdrew three pieces of white jade, the size of pigeon's eggs. He rolled them between his fingers, his mouth turned down in a wry smile.

It was a neat trick, demonstrated by a venerable Chinese musician whom Marie-Paule had met at a Cercle Français banquet earlier in the year. Lidiia, her on-again off-again girlfriend, had insisted they attend despite the morning's botched interview with the Shanghai Orchestra. Perhaps it had been naïve to think her inability to speak the language would be overlooked. Although the kind gentleman with the unpronounceable name had offered to provide a reference for the Conservatory of Music, she had not pursued the lead, grateful for the number of gifted pupils available to a good "European" teacher through advertisement. Henry, for instance. She tousled his strawberry-blond hair.

Alastair removed an embroidered face towel from an interior pocket and mopped his brow. "During the night, twenty-eight Japanese warships anchored near the mouth of the Huangpu." When agitated, his lips made this irritating pop-pop sound. "They landed troops on the east side, by the sea." He delivered this news without popping once, no doubt chastised by her look of distaste. "It has become dangerous for foreigners. You must leave immediately."

Marie-Paule had no intention of leaving. There had already been skirmishes between their hosts and the Japanese. No need to push off on the first ship that came along. Hadn't someone mentioned similar crises in 1927 and 1932? Shanghai's southern district was controlled by a council, appointed by the consul who reported to the Ministry of Foreign Affairs in France. She liked living in the French Concession, its streets shaded with leafy plane trees, and how fortunate to have found a shikumen rental. The skinny rowhouse charmed her still: its elaborately carved lintels, the bluish-gray brick, the dogleg staircase leading to a cozy bedroom, the box-style bed. Why, her forecourt even boasted a small garden, planted with ancient boxwood, three well-trimmed bushes that had woven their branches together like children holding hands.

"Refugees are pouring into the city." Alastair wiped his brow again. "There's no time to lose. Accompany me to the docks."

"I'm certainly touched by your concern but thank you, no. I plan to stay."

Marie-Paule had chosen her words with care, lest he take offense. She collected her wide-brimmed straw hat and ruffled parasol. Squinting against the sun's glare, she pushed open the metal gate that led to the shikumen's central lane and beckoned to Henry. Together they hurried through the stone archway on to the Rue Frelupt. Coolies called to each other, bicycle bells shrilled, dogs barked. A peddler with milk in baskets suspended on a shoulder pole stopped to wipe away sweat. Shanghai was full of life and eager to show it. She loved the animation, the intermingling of races, the implicit guarantee that they could all live together in harmony.

A chauffeur-driven car pulled up behind Alastair's Bentley. Henry gave a wave. Her next pupil wasn't due until four. After that came massage with Toshi, her Japanese masseuse, followed by another perm at La Bella Donna in the International Settlement. Perhaps she should let the bob grow out and request a trim instead? "Shi fu!" she called as Alastair joined her. "Be a love. Fetch me a runner."

"What do you intend to do?"

"Why, go see for myself."

They both looked past the Art Deco building toward the line of men squatting beside their rickshaws. Head back in genuine distress, he set off for the intersection. Could it be no one had told him the Japanese made trouble every five years? The sword-rattling would end after a week or two.

His panic reminded her of an incident at the Catherine Institute for Young Ladies of Nobility in Petrograd. On a frigid Sunday in March, she had been reading *Anna Karenina* in the lounge, snuggled under a blanket, when shouts rang out. The school's adults ran in all directions. She heard screams and the clopping of horseshoes on the cobblestone quay. More shouts, followed by a crash and the Fontanka Canal ice cracking as a heavy object fell in. Maids hefted mattresses down the stone staircase and propped them against windows while the headmistress herded the girls into two classrooms on the second floor and explained there was another revolt going on. No one called it a "revolution" yet.

That spring, a few days before her eighteenth birthday, the Bariatinskys escaped to France. They settled in Auteuil, in the same building as her mother's childhood friend who insisted on free violin lessons. With Parisian pals calling her Marie-Paule rather than Maria Pavlovna, she adopted the new name and used it on her application for a Nansen passport.

Her world changed again in 1930: travel to the Far East as assistant to a famous Russian pianist, marriage to said pianist, pregnancy, motherhood. Details she kept to herself. Japan had been a disappointment. Her foreign origins had complicated making friends. Shanghai was more to her taste, less staid, more vibrant. Around ten thousand White Russians had moved to the French Concession after the revolution and subsequent civil war. She rejoiced in the closeness of the blue-domed Orthodox Church and socialized with members of its congregation, former naval officers from Vladivostok and their daughters for the most part. Many of the stateless émigrés were desperate to marry, but not Marie-Paule. She preferred the single life.

Alastair, who had plodded halfway to the intersection, did a stiff about-face.

With a quick backward glance to verify his progress, she entered the house, kicked off her heels, and poured a glass of Watsons mineral water. The carved-wood kitchen god, lacquered red, then black, acquired in the Cercle Français raffle, smirked at her from its perch above the cabinet where she stashed the Cognac. In front of its ears were remnants of braided human hair.

Alastair shoved the front door open. "Don't you understand? I'm trying to save you here."

What a hard one to discourage. She had no intention of
moving to Australia. France, Japan, China. Three new countries were enough. She had enjoyed being escorted around
Shanghai by a successful businessman, whose attentions did
not require emotional commitment, rather than one of the
young dandies at the annual Russian ball, known to steal
hearts, but it was time to end the relationship.

"I'm sorry if I led you on," she said, compelled to honesty
by his despair. There. She'd said it. Apologized. Now for the
part that always worked: the truth. "Australia is out of the
question. I'm married."

Alastair raised his bushy eyebrows in disbelief. "What in
heaven's name does that mean?"

"I have a son. He lives with his father in Japan."

She fiddled with one of the mother-of-pearl buttons on
her silk blouse. The blouse was emerald, the color of her eyes.
Above their heads, the ceiling fan whirred. The mynah bird
ruffled his feathers. While the bird made obnoxious kissing
noises, Alastair stomped over to the Courvoisier cannon and
tucked the unopened bottle of Cognac into the crook of his
arm. His cheeks had become blotchy, white on red. "Juice not
worth the squeeze, hmm?"

It was probably difficult for him to fathom how she could
have left a son behind, a decision that pained her still. Being
a mother had proven messy. Who knew what her five-year-
old might do next? Vania's antics during afternoon tea at the
American Embassy had been such an embarrassment. What
an idea, to climb into a reflecting pool.

Marie-Paule felt vindicated by conversations with Henry Townley's mother, who confirmed Shanghai was no place to raise a child. Vania enjoyed a far healthier life in the mountains of Japan. Yes, he was better off in the company of his nanny and a doting father who taught him French and Russian. She could go visit. The overnight ferry left for Nagasaki three times a week.

The gate squeaked open. Marie-Paule's cook hobbled in, thin arms tight around a live chicken. "Please Missy," Ah Zee said, wide-eyed. "Cook chicken tomorrow. 'Bamboo wireless' say go home."

There was a loud explosion somewhere to the east, close to the Bund. At the first unmistakable drone of bombers overhead, Ah Zee fled, elbows angled out, hands clasped to her mouth. The chicken scuttled into the lane after her.

"What did I tell you?" Alastair snorted. "They're building shelters underground in Chongqing. Looks like you may need them here too."

It was highly unlikely that anyone would bomb the French Concession, which enforced its own laws. If he had counted on bullying her into submission, he had failed. She extended her hand, teeth barred into what she hoped would be read as a smile, and dismissed him with two words: "Alastair, adieu."

The Japanese occupied Shanghai in the fall. Although Marie-Paule managed to retain a few pupils from wealthy families, she decided to work several hours a day at Lidiia's shop on the Avenue Joffre, where she didn't have to pay for heat and could reward herself with undergarments, sold to employees at a discount: glamorous silk teddies, slips, panties, nightgowns.

Two years later Hitler invaded Poland, and the Second World War began.

2.

A rooster's crow rang through the shikumen complex wel-
coming the new day: April 1, 1943. It was Lidiia who introduced Marie-Paule to Dmitrii, an infectious diseases doctor
born in Vladivostok. She tried not to move as she lay in his
arms, and it occurred to her that the important events of her
life all seemed to take place during those first few weeks of
early spring, which her former cook called the time of the pale
green light. She thought back to 1939, when her husband traveled to China for a concert, a divorce, and her Amati—he had
promised to sell the precious violin if necessary. That same day
Ah Zee had dropped by with the traditional green dumplings.
She was heading to her village to sweep the tombs of ancestors
during the Qingming festival. Marie-Paule's ancestors were
buried on the grounds of the Alexander Nevsky Monastery in
St. Petersburg—renamed Leningrad by the Communists—
not a city she would visit any time soon with her family black-
listed. A year ago, wonderful, gangly Dmitrii had come into
her life. She loved his deep baritone, the prominent veins on
his expressive hands, the urgent way he made love.

Dawn slid its rosy fingers above the blackout curtains and
across the ceiling. Gradually the light illuminated the bottle of
Vol de Nuit he had given her the night before. The spicy vanilla
scent lingered. A red oil lamp burned under the icon of Mary
and baby Jesus hanging in a corner. Waves of heat rose from
the space heater. It had been a cold week, with a sprinkling of
snow. Shanghai snow wouldn't last. Never did. So much of this
world was temporary: the scrapes on her son's knees, morning
dew, ice cubes crackling in a glass of iced tea, the love of a governess fired by one's parents, luck, both good and bad.

When she turned her head back to the man at her side, he was watching. How she hated the idea of losing him. There could be no more procrastination. She would tell him today. Marie-Paule looked directly into those gentle eyes—one brown, one blue—and held his gaze, an eyebrow raised like Rita Hayworth, in case he was interested in "morning thunder," but he tapped his watch face twice and swung his feet to the floor, switching on the lamp below the corkboard, where she kept her map of Europe. Red pins indicated Red Army victories over the Wehrmacht. Only yesterday they had argued over his plan to return to Russia. He was convinced the Soviet Union needed specialists, that the country would want him back, despite rumors to the contrary. Foolish man. Communism stifled criticism and crushed independent thought. He'd find himself in a political rehabilitation camp. That's what happened to Lidiia's cousin.

Dmitrii ran his pointer finger over her aquiline nose, across her winter-pale cheeks, and down to circle the mole between her breasts, intent on drawing back her attention. He whispered a few words into her hair and wound a few strands around his finger.

"Couldn't you skip work and stay?" She bit her lip. What a selfish thing to say. Of course, he couldn't. When life knocks you sideways, all you can do is pick yourself up and continue your journey alone. Dmitrii had left the contents of his pockets on a side table. He draped her shawl over her narrow shoulders, collected his coins, his pipe, and the pocket watch set to Vladivostok time, two hours earlier. She stood up and laid her head against his shoulder, breathing in his cinnamon scent, the remains of an essential oil from Sri Lanka applied daily to counteract the risk of infection.

"Dushenka, accompany me to Vladivostok."

"Out of the question," she replied in a steely voice.

There was a knot in her throat as she listened to him reminisce about their homeland. The fact that Russian soldiers had been victorious at Stalingrad didn't signify the war's end. Say the government allowed Dmitrii to work. Assignment to a hospital in his hometown was doubtful. A return to Russia would be risky for them both. Who knew what might happen to someone with her background? The rumors were terrifying. Lidiia had heard the Soviet regime called members of the nobility "former people." Their children were denied an education.

"What will become of you, my stubborn darling? Friends at church say returning emigrants are sent to Siberia."

She understood his longing for wide-open spaces. It created a permanent ache that hurt more at the approach of spring. Whenever a balalaika played at Kavkaz, their favorite nightclub, the Motherland called. Marie-Paule had learned to adjust to exile, but dreams transported her back to Russia. Sometimes she gave in to the nostalgia. Wrapping herself in a blanket of memories eased the pain: the linden trees on her family's country estate, the excitement at her annual name's day party, the kind British governess who had urged young Marie-Paule to vocalize her feelings. Even today she could recall Miss Pritchard's perfume: so feminine, balancing jasmine and rose with vetiver, wintergreen, and a spicy touch of carnation.

"Don't be a numbskull," she cried out.

Up went her hands to hide her face. If only they would stop trembling. An inch of Cognac remained in her glass. The amber liquid burnt as she drank it down.

Mama and Papa would never approve of a man with no pedigree, from Vladivostok of all places. She turned away, trying to compose herself. A consolatory voice took over in her head: *Loss isn't new to you. You can learn to forget Dmitrii. This pain, too, will end.*

Marie-Paule hummed a few bars of a flute concerto by Beethoven and grasped her pearls. In one of his first letters, Vania had mentioned flute lessons. Perhaps it was a melody he played by now. Love for her son had become the only constant in her life. She looked forward to their reunion once it was safe to travel.

"Mitia, I have a son," she said in a lower pitch. "He lives with his father in Japan."

"Oh, my goodness!" squawked the mynah bird.

Marie-Paule picked up the red silk throw from the floor and threw it over the wicker cage before daring to assess Dmitrii's reaction. His angular face showed skepticism. Tears glistened in his luminous eyes, pooled on the eyelashes. Having him as a lover had made her miss Russia all the more.

"So, you're what? Married?" he said with an edge to his voice.

"Divorced. The thing is I need to be near my boy. He'll be thirteen next week."

"You said no secrets. No secrets, Maria. And I believed you."

"I've told you everything else," she murmured, although that wasn't true.

For years keeping certain matters to herself had offered protection from unwanted scrutiny. Why mention that she had been born a princess? Who cared about former wealth or rank in society? She pressed the pads of her fingers to the moist windowpane and held them there until her hands grew cold. Her nails were in desperate need of a manicure, an indulgence she could no longer maintain. She had gotten into the habit of observing children at play at French Park. A peaceful place. That's where she'd go later.

Dmitrii stroked her cheek but said not a word. She collapsed onto the sofa, drew her knees up to her chest, and didn't budge as he dressed in multiple layers—silk shirt, trousers, fitted jacket, overcoat, scarf, leather gloves.

She would not cry. Crying was a sign of weakness.

Soon it would be the time of the pale green light. There would be new beginnings. The grass would green up and buds would cover the magnolia. Joss paper would litter the streets. Over the next few days, she would allow herself a short period of mourning, the time it took to adapt to changed circumstances. Marie-Paule felt as if she were constantly reinventing herself and wondered whether it was a malady that afflicted other Russian émigrés or was hers alone. She sat head cushioned on her knees, anticipating the silence of solitude. Dmitrii yanked open the door, crossed the garden, and disappeared into the crowd.

3.

People are cheerier when the sun is shining, Marie-Paule said to herself on a brilliant Shanghai morning in late March 1949. She could sense spring in the air and planned to go for a walk after the embroidery session. Her new identity card was snug in her purse. She never left home without it. Ever since the Nationalists seized control of the French Concession's municipal governments, she had made a conscious effort to obey the law. Foreigners no longer held jobs in the police force or in utilities or at customs. The city had changed. Lost much of its glamour. And everyone was talking about Communism. People said Shanghai would soon fall.

Sunshine streamed in through the parlor window. She held her emerald blouse up to the light. The silk had a slight sheen, but the elbow stitches were neat and regular. Knowing how to sew had proven more useful than Russian literature or mathematics. Zheng excelled at mathematics. That had been a curious benefit of their relationship. He explained inflation and how to use an abacus, a skill Lidiia encouraged. He also taught her the correct pronunciation of useful phrases in the local dialect—five tones, not four. They had met at Lidiia's rose-scented shop. Zheng, who spoke impeccable French, left with a peach-colored teddy after asking her opinion on a lace negligee. One of his servants had shown up at the end of the afternoon with an invitation to dinner. Zheng owned a restaurant. He insisted on paying their way wherever they went, and she appreciated the largesse with only one pupil left. For six months, they had spent every Tuesday together.

Early on, Lidiia had advised accepting invitations from members of the expat community only. Not that it mattered anymore. Everyone of importance socially had left. Marie-Paule had sold most of her possessions: her jewelry, her Victrola, even the seventeenth-century kitchen god, which turned out to be quite valuable. It had warded off evil spirits for a dozen years. She used to tease Zheng that he resembled the antique statue with his hair loss at the temples and enigmatic expression that conveyed no emotion whatsoever. "Don a high-collared, long-sleeved robe with a cummerbund and that's you," she had said. With Zheng around, she felt less vulnerable, more serene. She'd miss those long, delicate fingers peeling bills off a roll of yuans. From the day he filled her courtyard with fragrant yellow tree peonies she had suspected black market connections, problematic should the Communists come to power. There. Another reason for immediate action. The first was his gambling. She couldn't tolerate the idea of an addiction. What's more, gambling led him to neglect her. End the relationship. Reunite with beloved Vania. Two steps, now clear in her mind.

Marie-Paule had already filed a visa application at the Canadian consulate. She hadn't told either Lidiia or Zheng. Instead, she informed her former husband who had sent a brief note to let her know their son was to attend college in New England. In her mind, he remained that rambunctious five-year-old with cowlick and turned-up nose. Vania would have to forgive her egotism. That's what it amounted to if truth be told. Abandoning your child. Allowing him to be raised by others. Gaining sexual independence but losing a son.

She laid her blouse in the dresser drawer beside his seven letters with their lush Japanese stamps showing mountains and waterfalls. From the closet she lifted her fan-shaped reed broom. Her sweeps were unhurried and methodical. There was satisfaction to maintaining order. She replaced the broom on its hook when the squeaky gate alerted her to the arrival of guests.

Zheng stood outside. An older woman was half-hidden behind him. She wore a figure-hugging *qipao* with a high cylindrical collar. Marie-Paule recognized the slender woman as Zheng's mother. She met the world with the same cautious eyes. "Niang" was what he called her. During their only other meeting, she had implored Marie-Paule to make him give up gambling. The expert mahjong player wanted her son to renounce his hobby.

"Marry me," he said without preamble.

Marie-Paule froze, uncertain how to receive this proposition. Only five days had passed since he humiliated her, off with friends at Damian's, a Jessfield Road nightclub whose owner supplied sensuous cigarette girls to entertain rich patrons. He had missed their Tuesday appointment. Although she might enjoy their conversations and lovemaking, it was time to move on.

A reluctant player in their little drama, Zheng's mother removed the bamboo pipe from her mouth and coughed. From the puffiness of her face, Marie-Paule sensed disapproval of his interest in a European, too old to produce grandchildren.

Zheng pulled an ivory box from a pocket of his loose-fitting black silk trousers. He flipped the latch. Marie-Paule saw herself obliged to examine what lay inside.

"You should try it on," he said, slipping the cabochon jade ring off its satin bed and onto her finger. "I asked Niang to come so there will be no doubt about my intentions." The three of them stood there, heads bowed, admiring her hand. "Keep the ring while you think it over."

She brought the hand up to her neck where her pearls used to be. Think it over? What was there to think about?

4.

By the middle of July, Marie-Paule felt desperate to leave Shanghai. Most of her friends had fled. Some had chosen the Philippines, others South America. If only her visa request would come through. Argentina wasn't her first choice by any means. She would have been in New England by now if not for Canada's newly enacted law that limited immigration from the Orient. Zheng had promised to pay for passage on a South American liner. They still met once a week. He had started asking for the ring back.

For years, she had stoically maintained that the turmoil in China was bound to end at some point. Until a few weeks ago that is, when the People's Liberation Army marched into the city. Her neighbors had hung red flags out their windows. Students stood on street corners, preaching the Red doctrine. Not that they harassed her in any way. The change had been subtle, a shift in perspective that made her realize foreigners were no longer welcome.

Her feet ached. She checked the travel clock Lidiia kept in a drawer. Almost closing time. The tissue paper rustled as she unpacked a shipment from France. She buried her face in a pair of silk panties, rubbed the fabric between her fingers. Touching luxurious lingerie remained such a comfort. She'd miss the texture of silk against skin.

It happened to be her birthday. Fifty years old and what had she accomplished? Her teacher in Paris would be disappointed. He had nicknamed her "the gifted one." She should have obtained a tenured position in an orchestra or be sharing her passion for music at a music conservatory, rather than folding underwear.

Two stylish young women browsed through the taffeta petticoats.

"Excuse me, Miss," the taller customer called in bad French. She had applied too much rouge. The higher slit on her *qipao* and nylon stockings spoke of affluence. "Could you help me locate your full slips?"

Marie-Paule gestured toward the far wall. The nouveau riche of Shanghai craved sexy lingerie. The fashion industry had taken advantage of a post-war yearning for frills, such stark contrast to the austerity in China, convulsed by civil war.

She raised her eyes when the sleigh bells at the top of the glass door jangled again to admit a foreign gentleman. His clothing spoke of a life of leisure in Paris, Rome, or Milan: a seersucker double-breasted suit with wide notched lapel, a brassy bow tie, a mauve silk square at the breast pocket. With expediency, he strode up to the counter and spoke in Russian. "Princess Maria Pavlovna?"

Few people in Shanghai knew her patronymic, let alone the fact that she had a title. The man clicked his heels and bowed his head. He was close to her age, and, judging from his heft, well nourished, not typical for the Russians left in the city. Who was this stranger, smelling of bergamot, with his old-world formality?

"I've come to inform your Excellency that you're on a list for deportation to the Soviet Union once the Communists take Shanghai."

She grasped the brass bar along the counter. Her breath came in gasps. The Communists were after her? Why maintain a blacklist after all these years?

"You leave for San Francisco tomorrow on the USS General Meigs."

"I only have a Nansen passport."

"Doesn't matter."

"No visa, no money."

"Many without visas will be on board. You'll receive a temporary stipend upon arrival in California." He started for the door.

"Wait!" A smile played on her lips for the first time in days. She felt every pore in her body come alive. "Tell me. Who am I to thank for this generosity?"

"Suffice it to say that I come on behalf of the Russian American Aid Association. They'll be glad to know I located you in time." He clicked his heels and was gone.

As the door swung shut, she let herself cry, warm tears of relief and gratitude.

That evening, Marie-Paule filled her lungs with the fetid breeze off the Huangpu. Before bed she finished the remaining bottle of Cognac and packed her suitcase, securing Vania's letters in the mesh pocket. She cut up one of her faded silk blouses and carefully sewed a tiny pocket into the waistband of her best skirt. She slid Zheng's ring inside. There was no way to return it to him now. She'd sell the ring once the stipend ran out.

In the morning, Marie-Paule shimmied into several layers of undergarments, wrapped her head in a turban, and spritzed her neck with the last quarter inch of Vol de Nuit. Outside, she let her hand linger on the carved lintel above the door. Her eyes caressed the boxwood hedge. She'd miss the joy of greeting the first foliage on her peony trees during the time of the pale green light when the garden first came alive. She'd miss her former hairdresser at La Donna Bella, who had promised to take good care of the mynah bird. She'd miss Lidiia. The gate squeaked as it swung shut one last time.

"Shi fu!" Marie-Paule called, summoning a rickshaw. "Shi fu!"

"La Petite Boche"

Through a crack in the cellar wall, I can see the night sky and choose a twinkly star for my wish that Papa returns to Leipzig now the war is over. I climb down from the empty jelly cupboard, slapping dirt off my hands. I'll forgive him providing he comes home. The hunger wasn't his fault, nor the bombing. I promise not to complain about his having named me after the tsar's youngest daughter, though I would have preferred a pretty name like Hildegarde or Kerstin. As I crawl across the floor, one of my sisters stirs in her sleep. I fluff my floppy-eared bunny, place it under my head, and shut my eyes.

I sleep soundly because no bombs fall during the night.

In the morning, I climb back up on the jelly cupboard. To my surprise, I see boots, and, above the boots, tan uniforms, not gray like the Nazis wear. The trapdoor is open. My big sister Kseniia comes halfway down the ladder. We have different fathers. Hers was an Orthodox priest who died before Mama and Papa met, something called "intestinal occlusion." She sticks out her tongue. It's brown as if Sophie and Lianka, our twin sisters, had convinced her to eat a mud pie.

Kseniia beckons with her fingers. "Chocolate bars, hurry."

The twins climb the ladder and dash outside. Mama and I follow, stepping around lumps of plaster. Mama wears her checkered kerchief but has put on a pretty dress, the blue dress with white polka dots. Somehow the bombing missed our street. Down at the far end, the funny round steeple of

Nordkirche is right where it should be. When buildings are bombed, they become piles of stones. These stones are called rubble. That's what Kseniia told me. There's rubble all over the city now.

Sophie hands me a chocolate bar. I peel off the wrapper and take a bite. A soldier tosses two more at my feet. The bar tastes like the bonbons from the candy shop where my grandmother—Babu—goes after church. I eat every bit. It has the consistency of a candle.

"Mine didn't melt in my hand," Lianka says in Russian, the language we speak at home.

I slip the third chocolate bar into my pinafore pocket.

"Two is enough, Nastia. This is no time for tummy aches." Mama takes a tube of lipstick from her purse and runs it over her lips, the bright red lipstick she let me play with in France.

At the gymnasium, Kseniia has learned to make sense of things, even chaos: "So, how do we tell these are the Allied troops?"

I pretend to leave the room but stand near the door to eavesdrop. First, Mama tells Kseniia about the jeep with the American flag. "Thank goodness the Yankees are here," she says. "I've heard dreadful rumors about the Red Army. The Soviet troops rape women . . ."

I miss the rest since she has lowered her voice. Here's what I made of her explanation. Some Allied troops are from the United States of America, and some are from the Soviet Union of Russia. The Nazis have lost the war. They're the bad Germans, who hired Papa as interpreter three years ago. It seems there are bad Russians too. They work as soldiers for a Red Army.

Several tanks go by in a cloud of dust. The dust settles on our clothes, our faces, our eyelashes. When the breakfast bell rings, the twins and I march into the house, swinging our arms. The house smells of porridge. Mama must have purchased oatmeal the day she sold her jewelry.

After breakfast, I go back outdoors and kick my feet sideways in a happy dance, which makes Sophie and Lianka giggle. They sit cross-legged on the stoop, intent on a game of jacks. The twins look less alike since Lianka has changed into a clean pinafore and brushed out her blond hair. They have greenish-blue eyes like Mama, but one of Sophie's eyes wanders. That's how to tell my sisters apart.

It isn't long before Kseniia joins us. Her glasses have broken. She's trying to repair them, this time with adhesive tape from our first aid kit.

"My tummy's happy." I rub it in a circle. "Porridge tastes as good as cream puffs."

"Not surprising. After all those raw potatoes."

We stand there together, taking in the sun's warmth.

"What does rape mean?"

She shakes a finger at me.

"Tell me, Kseniia."

"The Russian soldiers do bad things to women. We need to be afraid of them."

I decide I had better tell Heidi, my first-ever best friend. She lives across the street. Her dad is a prisoner in Tunisia. That's in Africa. Heidi helped me learn German. We played house together and chased butterflies. What we didn't do was talk about how much we missed our fathers.

We hear boots again and hold our breath until uniforms appear. Not tan or gray. Greenish brown. We exchange glances. These new soldiers will not be friendly like the chocolate men.

Mama stands in the doorway, clutching the gold cross around her neck.

"Could the Americans have left?" Kseniia asks.

"They must have been passing through. This is not good news. Not good at all."

I keep behind the gate because the soldiers are scary with their slanted eyes and dirty faces. Some ride horses. Others sit in wooden carts. They wear hats with flaps that cover their ears. I start running across Nordstrasse to warn Heidi, but one of the horses rears up and almost kicks me.

"Ostorozhno!" the rider yells.

I know what that means: watch out. Mama says ostorozhno a lot. I take a giant step backwards into the garden, toward safety.

*

Our garden reminds me of a game we used to play. You hold a buttercup under someone's chin to find out whether she likes butter. It seems like a strange game now there has been no butter for months. Or jam. Or honey. I pick some butter-cups anyway and run inside to hold them under Mama's chin. She clicks her tongue at me and pushes my bouquet away. Our suitcase lies open, half filled with clothing.

"Get ready, Nastia," she says, splashing on cologne which makes the house smell like lily-of-the-valley rather than por-ridge. "We're leaving for Nice."

"Let me draw a picture first, so Heidi knows where we're going."

I skip into my room for the colored pencils Papa sent for my seventh birthday. There's a Roman soldier on the box. I memorized Papa's note: *Draw me the world, Golubchik.* He calls me Golubchik, "little pigeon." Mama says he told her I looked like a bird as a baby, what with my dark eyes. I hope Papa can join us in France.

Babu lives in a white house on a hillside. She likes to sit on the front steps and soak her feet in an enameled basin. I draw the gate and the apricot trees growing beside it. The fig trees have big leaves and pear-shaped fruit. I use brown for the branches and pink for the figs. The roof is orange. The gate, turquoise. The mountains, in the distance, are blue. In the corner, I draw the sun with a face and a grin since the sun is always shining on the Cote d'Azur. And, of course, I draw myself between Mama and Papa and make sure we're holding hands.

Babu will be proud of me. There's this one thing she says: "Better is the poor man who walks in his integrity than the rich man who is crooked in his ways." It means be honest and don't tell lies. I haven't told any lies since we left France.

More tanks rattle by. I can see black smoke through the window. Kseniia was wrong about the fighting being over. That's the thing with war. You never know if it's over or not.

Mama yanks open the bedroom door. "Put on comfortable clothes. Two layers. Bunny, where did you leave Bunny?" She keeps flexing her fingers like when Papa left for Berlin, what Kseniia called "our days of tribulation," those awful months when Mama cried all the time.

I fetch Bunny from the cellar. Back in the kitchen, I touch the chocolate bar in my pocket and decide to save it for Heidi. Kseniia is taking the silver service from the drying rack. She dumps spoons into a satchel. It bulges like the neighbor's cat's tummy before the kittens were born. I make my voice loud enough to be heard over the clatter. "An envelope for my letter, please."

I follow Kseniia into the parlor, where she grabs an envelope from the desk.

Here's what goes into the satchel first: the photo of Babu, not because it's Babu in her Court dress but because of the frame. What I like is the squiggle of pretend ribbon on top. Mama says you can tell a Fabergé by the details.

Mama stands on a stepladder, unhooking our icon. She wraps it in a dishtowel. Kseniia jerks several pull cords from the drapes. She ties them around the smaller suitcase we brought from Nice, makes knots, creating loop-handles. Mama is now busy searching through a desk drawer. She tucks a slip of yellow paper into her pocket before shoving a second sweater at me. Kseniia helps me put it on. My refusal to let go of either the envelope or my pencil box means it takes forever.

Our sisters wait for us in the front hall. Lianka clasps Sophie's doll. Its arm is broken. Lianka had a doll too, exchanged for bread and cheese because of its perfect condition, "a necessary sacrifice" I heard Mama tell Kseniia. Lianka cried when she found out, so Sophie gave her Agnes. The dolls were presents from Papa.

Back in the kitchen, Mama switches off the Primus stove and dunks a hand towel into the hot water, "Let's become sparkle-clean, my darlings." Her voice rings with the joy of resuming a ritual. We haven't been able to wash in days. Days? Weeks.

Finally, she signals for safe-journey prayers. We all sit down the way Papa taught us. I bow my head and pray. Lianka gets to stand first because she's the youngest.

Mama replaces her checkered kerchief with a felt hat, jams in a hatpin, and thrusts her arms into the sleeves of her raincoat, though it's sunny outside.

I feel sad to be leaving Heidi. Maybe she can come visit.

"Let's hope we can still travel by train," Mama says to Kseniia.

"What if they bombed the station?"

"We must put ourselves in the hands of the Lord."

She makes the sign of the cross and leads us into the yard. I go in the opposite direction, across the street. Before dropping the envelope into Heidi's letterbox, I add the chocolate bar and run back so fast I crash into Kseniia, who clutches her satchel under one arm. The loop-handles make it easier to carry the suitcase. Mama grasps Lianka by the wrist, clicking her tongue, and we march down the alley. It felt like we were participating in some parade.

*

Kseniia was right about the station being bombed, but there's a freight train on the outermost track, which Mama calls a miracle. I bat at the smoke from the locomotive. A lady dressed in a long gray skirt and a white hat with a red cross in the middle stands beside the second boxcar. The sliding door is open. Her frizzy hair is pulled back in a bun.

"This is the last train out of Leipzig," she says with a sing-song accent that tells me she's not German. Swiss maybe? "We're evacuating women and children in priority." She presses a piece of nougat into my palm.

I let her hoist me into the freight train. The boxcar smells like the neighbor's stable, a musty smell of wood after rain. My sisters' eyes widen. They're probably remembering the sleeper car on the trip from France. A conductor folded the velvet seats into beds. The beds had linen sheets.

"You must be extremely quiet," the lady says. Bobby pins hold her funny white hat in place. "Can you do that, little girls?"

Mama asks, in French, about traveling without identity papers. The lady says not to worry about the Boche anymore because they have lost the war.

"Who are the Boche?" I whisper to Kseniia.

"It's a pejorative term for Germans."

"What does pejorative mean?"

"Insulting." Kseniia turns back to the lady. "Where is this train going?"

"Bavaria. If the Russians find you aboard, they'll show no mercy. They control half the countryside. Whenever the train stops, total silence. Understood?"

I stick my thumb in my mouth although I haven't sucked my thumb ever since I promised to stop on my birthday.

The boxcar has no seats or beds. Only straw.

"Find a place to sit," Mama says. "We must do our best to stay alive. Your father expects to see you." She bows her head and recites the Lord's Prayer.

My sisters and I have heard about fearing to *walk through the valley of the shadow of death* so often that none of us pay much attention. What I do notice is mention of Papa, a good sign. Perhaps our family will soon be reunited.

At each railroad crossing, Mama shushes us. We are stow-aways, she says. Stowaways ride trains without tickets. Anyone can be a stowaway after a war. Sometimes a train gets searched, sometimes not. We're hiding from the Red Army. The Reds haven't gone home yet and may not know it's time to stop fighting. Two families ride with us. Dieter is seven, like me. Dieter and his brother Gert have string to play Cat's Cradle.

I spend the night curled up in straw, lulled by the rocking of the boxcar. After a few hours, the train stops, waking us up. Outside, two men speak Russian. I form words with my lips—*go away, go away, go away*. Kseniia squeezes my hand as funny shadows from a lantern dance across the wall. Whatever the men do takes forever. With a jolt, the train starts up again.

In the morning, I take my turn in the corner, squatting to pee with thumb and finger to my nose. My tummy makes its hunger noises. Gert and Dieter are hungry too. Yesterday their mother guessed our destination. It's . . . Munich! I would have preferred Berlin because Papa promised to take me to the zoo with all the pink flamingos.

At last, the train enters a city. We hear the locking bolt slide to one side, and the boxcar door opens. At first, I don't know what to think because of all the skinny men on the platform. Some have bandaged arms or limp along on crutches. Those in charge wear tan uniforms, which means we're in the part of Germany that belongs to America. Two soldiers walk past speaking English. I jump out and land hard, scraping my knee. Mama says the doctors here are too busy for children with scraped knees.

"I'm going to be a doctor when I grow up," I tell her and think for a minute. "A doctor who cares for children with scraped knees as well as for wounded soldiers."

Oh, no. Bunny is missing! Mama refuses to let me go back. I also have forgotten to say goodbye to Dieter and Gert. I feel like crying.

Kseniia pushes me toward a huge iron pot. A soldier scoops watery spinach and mashed potatoes into metal bowls. The smell reminds me how hungry I am. I eat every spoonful.

Another soldier offers to help us find "transportation". We climb into a truck with canvas sides. The truck takes us to a "reception center." The reception center used to be a school. The Americans have piled desks in a corner and set up cots. Ladies show us where to sleep. I write a new word in my diary: refugee.

*

"Let's go, my darlings," Mama says after a breakfast of white bread and milk. "I asked permission to take you outside. We could do with some fresh air."

In my head, I start to play Follow the Leader with Mama as our leader. Off we go with the suitcase and the satchel and Sophie's one-armed doll and Mama's slip of yellow paper. Kseniia says to watch for a grocery. It's easy to walk because the ground is flat here. In the distance, we will soon see mountains, Mama says. She calls them "Alps." A few jeeps and military vehicles, filled with soldiers, drive past. We pass a church and a park with swings. Not a grocery in sight. We turn left at a sign for the Theresienwiese Steps. As we approach, I spot a man on a motorcycle. Mama drops our suitcase and shrieks Papa's name: "Andrei! Andrei!"

We stand in a row, looking up, and that's when it happens.

"Sophie-Lianka-Golubchik!" the man shouts and stumbles down the steps, waving his arms.

I try not to stare, since, at first, I have no idea who this wild person is. He grabs Sophie and swings her into the air. Then he's kissing Lianka. At my turn, I recognize the smell of his pipe tobacco. Sure enough, it's Papa, right here in Munich. My wish has come true. I feel like my heart might burst. Climbing on the jelly cupboard has paid off. I wait for him to kiss Mama, but he doesn't. I watch him wipe his eyes on a monogrammed handkerchief like the one I used to keep under my pillow.

"Why are you crying?" I ask.

"These are tears of joy, Golubchik. I thought you had been killed."

"We thought you were in Berlin." Kseniia frowns and mutters something about fathers who abandon their family.

Mama tells him about the soldiers with slanted eyes. Papa says they must be from a place called Mongolia. He has been interviewing Russian prisoners and will now work for the Americans, only he's under house arrest until the paperwork is signed. Mama must have known the address. Why didn't she let on? That piece of paper! Was it a telegram?

Papa lives a block away. Thank goodness we won't have to sleep on cots tonight. We can move into his big beautiful flat. Lianka and Sophie are holding hands, skipping along as happy as can be. There's a tricycle in the lobby, which makes me think a German family lives here too. Maybe the children are my age and will play with me. We follow him inside. The staircase smells of potato soup. Up we go to the second floor. The door to our new home is open. A woman in an apron stands at the stove, stirring laundry with a long wooden spoon.

"Girls, meet my fiancée," Papa says as she greets us. "Nina honey, these are my daughters."

I glance at Mama. Her eyes have narrowed like when she killed the mouse in our kitchen. I hear laughter from behind a curtain.

"And this is your brother. Time to come out, Pavlik. He likes to play hide and seek. It's his favorite game."

"Not ours," I say.

Mama doesn't want to meet Pavlik either. She's talking about identity papers and not having any and can't he help his own daughters for Chrissake and when is he going to give her money so we can continue our journey and Kseniia needs "protection from the curse," which means she's bleeding again *down there*. It turns out there's a Tante-Emma-Laden grocery around the corner. Nina volunteers to show us the way. Sophie and Lianka are each on one of Papa's knees. I just stand there, feeling like I want to spit up. Tears roll down my cheeks and they aren't tears of joy. With the war over, our family was supposed to get back together. I'm afraid that won't happen, not with Nina and Pavlik in the world.

*

Papa counts out the Deutschmarks we'll need. He has been talking about how great it will be to do his interpreting for the Americans. How his new job will make it easier to wire us money. How valuable interpreters are in time of war.

Nina has returned with a loaf of dark bread. Kseniia goes into the bathroom while I help make sandwiches to show Papa how grown-up I've become since he abandoned us.

Nina smears lard on five slices of bread, cutting off the crusts—Pavlik doesn't eat crusts. Once her back is turned, I sweep the crusts into my pinafore pocket. She also fills a thermos and offers to boil Kseniia's underwear. There's no soap, of course. She uses ashes. Mama says thank you very much, but no, we must be on our way.

"Don't underestimate the benefit of speaking multiple languages," Papa says and winks at Nina. "We met at the ballet in Berlin, a performance by Vitale Fokine."

Before joining Pavlik, Nina pats my head and I freeze up.

"Where are your manners, Golubchik? Give Nina and Pavlik hugs."

I scowl at the twins who do as Papa says. Kseniia is with me, halfway out the door. I'm angry with her, too, because she knew Mama's secret. All those conversations about pink flamingos in the zoo and Kseniia couldn't drop any hints, not a one?

Papa drives us to the station and buys our tickets. He gives instructions on what to do if people try to arrest us. He says everyone will be impressed because he's a duke and Mama's a duchess, but she's not supposed to tell until all hope is lost. I'm studying his thin blond hair to remember it better when he asks Sophie what happened to her doll.

"I've kept my colored pencils," I interrupt, speaking German. I hold out the Mars box with the Roman soldier.

"Splendid," Papa says in Russian. "Will you draw a picture of Babu's house and send it to me?"

I say I will but it's a lie. I have no intention of sending him a picture of Babu's house or anything else for that matter. Leipzig, Berlin, Munich. What if he has moved again and

I don't have the new address? For all I know, he might have changed wives by the time my letter reaches him. I'm having trouble breathing. I glance around at my sisters. We all have tears in our eyes.

*

We board a green train and speed along for a couple of hours. The train stops in Augsburg and Gunsberg. Mama tells us the next stop should be Ulm. Other stowaways crowd in with their bundles. Our compartment smells of sweat.

Ten minutes later, the train slows down in the middle of a field. Kseniia manages to open the window.

"Oh, no!" she cries. "The railroad bridge, it's been bombed."

"No bridge?" Mama says. "We'll have to walk."

"Walk?!" Sophie and I exclaim in unison. Lianka simply hangs her head.

As the eldest of Papa's three daughters, I fold my arms against my chest.

"I refuse."

"Oh, and perhaps Mademoiselle Anastasiia has a better suggestion?" Kseniia says in her don't-be-such-an-idiot voice.

She leaves me no choice: I stick out my tongue.

The other passengers push and shove. I don't know why they're in such a hurry. It's not like there's an express train waiting to pick us up.

Once outside, Kseniia speaks to a man with a bandaged head.

We accompany him for a while. His name is Luigi, and he was injured when a bomb hit the factory where he works. He's heading home to his village near Milan. That's in Italy.

At first, I'm afraid Red Army soldiers will find us, jumping out from behind trees or arriving at top speed on horseback, but Luigi tells me not to worry. Our destination is a place called Schaffhausen. That's in Switzerland, a country below Germany on our map of Europe. I imagine roofs made of chocolate and storks nesting in chimneys, like in the picture book Babu sent before the war stopped mail delivery. All we need to do is follow the trails, Luigi says. They cross meadows and forests and more meadows. His granddad took him camping here once. Mama says moss makes a fine mattress, better than our cellar floor. The second day, Luigi's leg starts hurting. He stops to rest in a deserted barn. I feel sad to leave him but not as sad as Kseniia. She blushes when I tease her about it.

My leg hurts too but Mama says to keep going. I wish I had time to draw the pretty landscape with all its wildflowers: lupines and daisies.

It isn't long before we stop carrying the silver spoons and Sophie's doll.

At our next rest stop, Mama removes Babu's photo from the frame. She leaves the frame beside a boulder with the suitcase. I agree to give up my pencil box. First the most useful colors, blue and red, go into my pocket. All we keep is our icon.

I decide to play some thinking games. First, I count to one hundred in German the way Heidi taught me. Next, I count backwards to zero. I do the same in Russian, which is much harder.

For a while we follow a group of refugees. Mama prefers that we keep our distance because they may have "vermin," which are nasty bugs, so we stay on the opposite side of the paved road. I keep my eyes peeled for Luigi, but he must have taken a different route.

We fill the Thermos in streams. If we spot a village, Kseniia runs to fetch bread. Once, she's able to buy a sweet loaf that tastes like kulich, the yeast bread Babu bakes at Easter. Mama and Kseniia talk about how Babu puts pillows around the pan as the dough rises. I'm imagining Babu teaching me to bake kulich when Mama claps her hands. A sign indicates we are about to enter Switzerland. We follow the arrows leading to a brick building marked Zoll/Douane. This is it! The border, at long last. We hug and jump up and down. Mama starts crying.

None of us can pronounce the town's name: Thayngen. It sounds like a sneeze. I practice, making my sisters laugh. "Thayngen, thayngen, thayngen."

"Identity papers please," the customs official says.

He shakes his head because we don't have any, not even what he calls a "Nansen" passport. I'm afraid he may not let us in. I don't know where he expects us to go, since we need to cross Switzerland to reach France. He speaks to another man who asks what we were doing in Leipzig if we're not German. Mama explains about Papa's interpreting job. The customs official doesn't believe her. He accuses us of trying to "immigrate." Kseniia says that we're on our way to Nice, which is the absolute truth.

"We can't wait to get there," I add and mention Babu's white house and describe the fig tree leaves: big as my hand.

I can tell Mama is fed up with this conversation because she starts flexing her fingers. She asks the men if they like history and brings up our ancestor who was married to Napoleon. Her name was Josephine. The customs officials listen to the story about how Josephine's grandson married a grand duchess who was Papa's grandmother. The man with the wart is smiling as he fills out a form printed in red ink.

Before we can enter Switzerland, we must be "deloused." Mama tells the men how careful she has been, but they insist. I hold my nose. The dust makes me cough.

Afterward, we board a train behind the border-crossing building. Thank goodness we don't have to walk anymore. I use my blue pencil to write down the names of the villages in my diary: Rafz, Huntwangen, Eglisau. Right after Bülach, we see the Alps again. At Zurich Central Station, we locate the train for France. Almost there!

In Nice, Mama hails a taxi. I'm excited because we're going to see Babu. Sophie has ripped her skirt. Mama says we look like Gypsies with our dirty clothes and what will Babu think? I don't say anything. I know how happy she will be. She won't care how we look.

The sun through the open window feels warm against my cheek. The air smells of nutmeg and tangerines. We drive up a hill to the turquoise gate and tumble out of the car. Babu rushes down the front steps to greet us. All I can think of is soaking my feet. Her dog Cadeau runs in circles. He's barking from the excitement.

"We made it, we made it," Mama repeats over and over.

"That was quite an adventure," Babu says after we tell her our story. "Don't forget a single detail. Tell your grandchildren."

A funny sound comes out of my mouth. All I want to do is forget. I miss Heidi. Her dad must be home by now. I miss Papa too but try not to think about him.

The neighborhood kids call me "la petite Boche" because of my German accent. I guess they don't realize I'm Russian. I won't let it bother me. Only one thing matters. The war is over and we're alive. I'm grateful for that.

For Dr. Natalie de Leuchtenberg Bowers

The Mother, the Daughter, and the Con Man

1.

The day Helena called to say she had moved to Brooklyn, the actor who played Alfalfa on *My Gang* was shot dead in an argument over a debt. I had been a fan, so the murder put me in a tizzy, and I was unable to finish Seascape 55, my latest attempt to capture the light that shimmers off the Inner Harbor. We were in 1959. Post-Stalin, pre-Nixon, before Khrushchev slammed his shoe onto a desk at the United Nations. I cradled the telephone to my shoulder, pouring myself another inch of gin.

"Grisha asked me to marry him," Helena said. "I can't believe my luck." Her voice swelled with happiness and a warning not to disagree. "He's good-looking, kind, rich. I have no intention of losing him."

Apparently she decided to move as soon as that Gregory fellow—Grisha!—proposed. What's a mother to say to such nonsense? At least we had been introduced, although Helena's beau didn't care much for Thanksgiving in Gloucester, not la-dee-da enough for his taste. Gregory told me he worked for jeweler Harry Winston and had negotiated the recent donation of the Hope diamond to the Smithsonian. He said he was born in a French castle. *Un château.* He paid in cash for our Union Oyster House dinner and knew all about Cezanne's Garçon au Gilet Rouge, sold at auction in London, where he maintained a house near North Square.

"But are you sure?" I stepped away from the easel. "Can you trust him?"

Recognizing truth has become more of a challenge since NBC dropped *21* amid irregularity allegations. It was my favorite quiz show. Although I would have preferred a big wedding for Helena, who am I to preach? I eloped at eighteen. Not such a good idea. Her dad left me when his dream job in Paris came through.

2.

"God, Mum. Pick up the damn phone." Where the devil can she be? That ridiculous soap she follows ended 10 minutes ago.

"Volkonsky Residence."

She enunciated the words in that precise way of hers. At least she hasn't been drinking. When I announced my engagement a week ago, her falling off the wagon became my greatest concern.

"Oh, Mum." My voice was a mess, and my hands shook.

"What are you doing?"

"Shoes, I'm sorting shoes!"

"You sound hysterical. What's happened?"

"It's Grisha. He's been sent to Rikers."

"Rikers Island?"

"The prison. They arrested him."

Mum said nothing. We sat in silence as if I had announced Khrushchev planned to drop a nuclear bomb on the city. With a half-sob, I recalled how idyllic everything had been at first, despite the apartment being a walkup. Earlier that morning, Grisha had palmed back his hair as he stepped out the door, one eyebrow raised.

I decided to summarize: "He left for work. Gave me a kiss first. I was unpacking my shoes. We got this special shoe rack at Macy's, the kind that fits over the door. Anyway, two hours later, the phone rings. It's his ex-wife's daughter Tiffany. Tiffany says he's at Rikers." I drew in a breath. "I need money for bail." The silence dragged on. "You there, Mum?"

"How did he get himself arrested?"

"Didn't show up in court. His ex says he owes her money. We've got to raise $3,000."

"Darling, now you listen closely. Throw those shoes of yours in a suitcase and get out of there. Leave now. Now!"

She was yelling at me. My mother, as gentle as Captain Kangaroo.

3.

This "house of detention" is a crazy place with sirens whining at odd times of the day and night. They've charged me with delinquency, not crime. Two fucking days ago. Of all times to be down on my luck. Helena was way beyond my wildest dreams. She believed whatever I dished up: the Hope diamond, the North Square townhouse, the yacht Uncle Ilya keeps in the Mediterranean. That part, about family from Russia, is the honest-to-goodness truth. I'm descended from royalty. My ancestors were loaded but not smart enough to stash the loot abroad. My old man drove a cab in Paris. I didn't ask Helena for help with the rent like that crumb-bag I married. Fuck her for setting the cops on me. You can't pay alimony you don't have. They allowed one phone call. Tiffany said she'd let Helena know. Maybe Mr. Bigshot Volkonsky can bail me out. I sure don't intend to stay in the slammer. My cellmate claims a plane crashed here two years ago. Some inmates got themselves freed by rescuing passengers. I'd do that in an instant. I'm a classy guy. Here's how I operate: I give women a phony business card. Tell them I'm a talent scout, that they'd be perfect for a role in our next film. A remake of *King Kong* or *Gone with the Wind*. Do they have a union card? When they say no, I pretend to phone my director friend. *SAG membership requires money, but I can handle it,* I say, all confident like. I wait outside while they're at the bank. Works like a charm. I didn't pull that on Helena though. The gal's a keeper. In case she can't raise the dough, I told Tiffany to call a buddy of mine. By sunset tomorrow, when those orange rays reflect off Manhattan, I'll be heading for the ferry slip, free again.

Hanky-panky

Prudence led such a sheltered life that she gasped when her parents accepted, on her behalf, an invitation to Connecticut, extended by a long-lost cousin who was practically a stranger. It was her dad's interest in genealogy that put the family in touch with Ivan, a brilliant, though slightly eccentric, scientist. At the time of Ivan's arrival in Baltimore, Prudence was in her bedroom, pasting photos from Screen-and-TV-Album Magazine into a scrapbook: Roger Smith, Gardner McKay, Sean Connery. The *From Russia with Love* photo showed Sean Connery kissing his co-star. Her parents sat downstairs in front of the television. Chet Huntley and David Brinkley were discussing the Democratic National Convention in Los Angeles. She heard them mention Senator Kennedy of Massachusetts and his wife Jacqueline. The doorbell rang. A few minutes later an unfamiliar female voice said something about a conference.

"Milk or lemon?" (That was her mom.)

"What conference?" (Her dad.)

"The International Electron Devices Meeting at the Shoreham Hotel in Washington, D.C." (A forceful male voice she did not recognize.)

"My husband does research . . . semiconductors . . . transistors . . ."

Transistors was the word that caused Prudence to close the scrapbook. For Christmas, she had requested her own transistor radio, a gift Song Hits Magazine stated every thirteen-year-old deserved to receive from Santa.

As she made her entrance, the guest helped himself to one of her mom's blown-glass ruby goblets, handcrafted in Sandwich, Massachusetts. Prudence observed the way he transferred hot tea from the Limoges teacup into the fragile ruby goblet. A dumb idea. It might break. For some reason his eyes followed her across the living room. She did not look away.

Her dad said, "Come meet my second cousin and his wife Mila."

She offered a quick curtsy, the traditional greeting in her household. Mila, who wore a dark blue maternity dress and a necklace of enameled Easter eggs, set down her knitting and shook hands with genuine warmth. Ivan was a short wiry man with round tortoiseshell glasses, brown eyes, a circle beard. A lot younger than her dad. She didn't mind having older parents but bristled at their old-fashioned parenting philosophy like, for instance, insistence on a chaperone for visits with Ashton, her boyfriend. Yesterday they had refused to buy her a bikini. Her friends owned bikinis or, at least, two-piece swimsuits.

Her mom did all the talking. She asked about life in Ridgefield, Connecticut. Were there community activities to join? Book clubs? Potluck dinners? She mentioned the schools Prudence had attended, their Schenley Road neighborhood, her younger brother, who was off playing Whiffle ball with a friend. At this point her dad lifted his album of vintage photos from the coffee table and started talking Russian history. It was the default topic of conversation at her house. Ivan picked up a framed photo of her famous grandfather, resplendent in full military regalia. He stared at it for a long moment before regaining his seat.

Prudence waggled the tips of her fingers and disappeared into the kitchen. She returned five minutes later with a Coke and a peanut butter sandwich. The conversation had developed into a debate on the benefits of multiple language proficiency.

Her mother went into detail about how the choice to study Italian at college had facilitated adaptation to Rome during an assignment for the Fulbright Program. "Always take into account the consequences of such choices," she concluded.

"We speak Russian to our children." Mila fixed her gaze on Prudence. "You'll hear Russian if you come visit this summer."

"Your parents gave permission," Ivan added. "What say you?"

Prudence considered her boring one-piece swimsuit. From her mom's startled expression, it was clear permission had not been granted. But so what? A one-piece wouldn't matter in another state because none of her eighth-grade friends would be there.

"Is there a pool?"

"No pool," Ivan said.

His dictatorial tone made the invitation feel like a dare. All eyes were upon her now. She shifted her weight from one foot to the other.

"Sure. I'm up for anything."

"But how will you get there?" stammered her mom.

"I can pick her up," Ivan said. "I return in August, on business."

"Will you drive?"

"No. I take the shuttle. Eastern."
And so, it was settled.

*

Prudence had never been away from home before, except for two sleepovers and a pajama party. The Russian cousins lived in an unremarkable house on a tree-lined street near the town center. Ivan made a detour past Woolworth's, ostensibly to made sure she saw the public pool, before driving five more blocks and parking beside a four-bedroom Colonial with a broken swing set in the side yard.

In the morning, Mila rang the breakfast bell at 7:30 sharp. Her three children sat ruler-straight at the kitchen table. Ivan's departure sparked coordinated chaos, punctuated by giggles. As soon as the beige Rambler sped off, eight-year-old Roksana and her younger siblings Sonia and Niko all chattered at once in English, despite Mila's reminders to speak Russian.

Prudence joined their mad games of hide and seek, played hopscotch with the girls, built tents between twin beds for four-year-old Niko, crawled around the floor in search of errant marbles. Ivan returned at 6 p.m. when the silliness ended and her little cousins dashed to the kitchen table, burying their heads in workbooks to prepare for "Russian" school. Mila tolerated this behavior with stoicism, albeit measured.

The next day Ivan returned home at noon. Prudence had organized a game of Dirt Detective in the back yard, and each child clutched a booty bag. Niko had filled his with dandelions. Sonia's contained a butterfly wing. Only Roksana understood the meaning of "digging for treasure" and had gathered stones for the rock collection she kept hidden in a stationary box under her bed: mica, coal, gray slag with bubble holes.

Ivan strode to the end of the driveway and tilted his head toward the car. "Let's go," he said.

"Go where, Cousin Ivan?"

"Local sightseeing. We'll start with my workplace."

Mila collected the children. Prudence could hear their protests as Ivan stepped on the gas. He drove to a boxlike building without windows. She pictured elves at workstations, toiling away, safety goggles snug over their eyes. There would be a conveyor belt, with a pastel-colored transistor radio at regular intervals, and the elves would hold soldering irons and high-speed drills.

Reality turned out to be far less whimsical. Engineers, at desks, waved as their boss escorted her through the electronics plant. Frumpy middle-aged secretaries said hello with nosy interest, which abated once Ivan identified her as *a distant cousin, here from Baltimore to help with the kids.* Not exactly the truth, at least not as she had understood it. In his office, he showed off a circuit board studded with transistors and said he had patented the design.

Their second stop was a camera shop in Stamford. The pervasive chemical smell, broken Venetian blinds, and dim lighting made her tense up. For all she knew they might be trespassing though Ivan had gained entry to the second-floor photography studio with a key. He removed a Leica from a drawer, flicked on two powerful spotlights, and patted a stool in front of a projection screen. From a box of props, he extracted a tired bouquet of fake mountain laurel.

"Your parents will want to know what we've been up to," he said.

Want to know what they'd been up to? Decidedly not. Her mom never left her alone with a man. But it was only Cousin Ivan, taking photographs. No cause for concern. She clutched the plastic flowers while he clicked away.

Before their return to Ridgefield, he developed the roll of film and let her join him in the dark room, where he explained the basic principles of photo enlargement. She had to admit it did feel good to be treated like an adult.

He didn't mention the photography session until Saturday after what were his regular darkroom hours. The whole family admired the enlargements. Prudence wasn't as smitten. Her freckles stood out against her pale skin. Her pores were enormous, like small craters. Roksana asked if she could have a photo. Her father refused. Prudence resolved to provide one later, in secret.

*

The family ate Sunday dinner in the dining room. The solemn meal proceeded in silence with Ivan shoveling food into his mouth, oblivious to his daughters who stared down at their plates, swinging legs under adult-sized chairs until he bellowed at them to sit still. Prudence ignored him, her mind on dessert. She and Niko had baked that morning during the two hours the family spent at church. What made her brownies superior was the addition of chocolate chips. She rushed to accomplish the distribution of dessert plates, all different, a tedious chore because each child had a "special plate"—a flower design or a gold rim. A quick look around the table revealed Sonia hadn't eaten her glazed carrots, Roksana picked at the creamed spinach, Niko wouldn't touch the liver with onions. Perhaps dinner wasn't finished, although Ivan had snapped open a Russian-language newspaper.

One arm around her pregnant belly, Mila pushed off the armrest. She produced a white blouse, stabbed with pins from her sewing basket. "The children love having you visit," she said. "Here's a little gift so you won't forget us."

"How could I forget you?" Prudence said, serving Niko the brownie with the most chocolate chips on top.

To her horror, a hairy hand shot out and seized her arm.

"*Niet*," Ivan said in a firm voice. "No dessert until he finishes supper."

An emptied plate was the rule for the offspring of many Russian immigrants. She heard often, at dinner, about the *unfortunate kids in Third World nations with nothing to eat* and yet her dad tended to compromise. A few bites sufficed to cool his ardor. Not Ivan. What a weird one, she said to herself. Monday through Friday and sometimes on Saturdays too, he wore the same charcoal gray suit with worn lapels. She felt both repulsed and attracted to this peculiar square-faced man who acted like he appreciated her company. How else to explain the guided tour of the electronics plant? He had spoken of his son with such pride after she picked up a snapshot of Niko from the cluttered desk. She cleared her throat. "Cousin Ivan, he helped with the batter. Can't he taste?"

"No spinach, no dessert."

Niko dug at the onions with a fork and sought out his mother's eyes for commiseration. Mila picked at the fringe on her apron, hesitant to take sides.

"That goes for you girls too," Ivan added.

This second warning made the food disappear fast. Sonia and Roksana gulped down every bit, lest his wrath bleed on to them.

Prudence resumed her seat in stunned silence. Why did Ivan treat his kids with contempt? It was a challenge to reconcile this attitude with his darkroom behavior. During the film processing demonstration, he had shown himself to be solicitous of her opinions. Considerate. Altruistic.

"I'm going on a business trip tomorrow," he announced from behind the newspaper. "How about you accompany me?"

"Will you be away long?" Mila asked.

"Two days. Upstate New York. It will do our guest good to see more of her country. What say you?"

Prudence blushed at realizing Ivan was addressing her. Why did she deserve special treatment? To say no would offend her host. All his decisions were final. She looked to Mila in time to see her eyelids crumple and close. When the eyes opened, it was as if a curtain had descended, thicker than the velvet drapes already pulled shut for evening.

*

In the morning, Prudence braided her hair into one long plait while listening to the girls' voices through the open window. Once ready to join them outside, she swung around and almost crashed into Mila who stood in the doorway. The older woman appeared to be sizing her up. Perhaps she had counted on childcare after all and didn't have the guts to say so.

"Can you keep an eye on Niko while I drop the girls off at ballet?"

"Of course. Am I going on that trip with Cousin Ivan?"

"You are. We'll have an early supper. How about you wear your new blouse? It's in our room. I sewed rickrack on the neckline. Rickrack adds *un je-ne-sais-pas-quoi.*"

Prudence liked the romantic sound of the French words. No one she knew talked like Mila, whose speech retained a certain crispness of pronunciation thanks to a British governess her parents had employed in the south of France. Ivan, on the other hand, spoke with an accent.

"Why was Cousin Ivan so strict yesterday?"

"What my husband can't stand is rebellion," Mila said.

Prudence had her doubts. Although he might be tough on Niko, she had seen compassion in Ivan's eyes when she commented on the snapshot at the electronics plant. Maybe the photograph reminded him of his own rebellious nature in childhood. She decided Mila must be mistaken. Rebellion was a quality her cousin admired.

"You don't mind, do you, if I leave for a couple days?"

Mila brushed glitter off her sleeve. "Why would I mind?"

Her fears allayed by this brief interchange, Prudence beelined for the master bedroom. Now, to dress appropriately for the business trip. First, she tucked in Mila's blouse and studied her reflection in the floor-length mirror. Too form-fitting. She pulled out the front ends, tied a bow, twisted her head this way and that. She had packed a half-empty tube of her mom's lipstick as blusher. Only after a couple dabs beneath her cheekbones did she feel satisfied with her appearance.

Downstairs, an empty tube of Walbead Sparkle Glitter remained on the coffee table beside a pile of library books. Niko climbed into her lap and Prudence read him *Make Way for Ducklings.* While she wracked her brain for more entertainment options, he threw a rubber ball behind the ugly TV console in a corner. She squeezed into the narrow triangular space to retrieve the ball and discovered a battered briefcase full of photos, grainy black-and-white photos of a blonde in a state of undress.

"We play catch outside," Prudence said in as firm a voice as she could muster. "Out."

Niko wiped the snot dribbling from his nose on a blue-checked sleeve and hopped off toward the sun porch. She leaned down to study the top photo more carefully. Perched on a stool, the blonde wore panties and a strapless bra. She tipped a derby hat or held a fan of fluffy white feathers. With her easy smile, the model—if that's what she was—seemed to have the confidence of a cheerleader.

The photos occupied her mind all morning. Who was the blonde? Did Mila know? Did she approve of her husband's hobby? Art photos, Prudence concluded. Possibly for submission to a contest. Taken at the photography studio. She'd seen the hat in a box of props. Yes. That was it. Thank goodness Cousin Ivan hadn't asked her to pose half naked.

That afternoon, she walked to Woolworths for the latest issue of *Seventeen*. She also bought a handful of fireballs.

At 5 p.m., Ivan arrived with a bouquet of red roses. Prudence was glad to see him kiss his wife goodbye. Mila's kiss was a shy peck on the cheek that he returned perfunctorily. Ashton's kisses were long and hard. That's the way she'd kiss her future husband, Prudence decided. Long and hard.

Evening traffic didn't ease up until the New York Thruway. Ivan had mounted a rectangular device on the dashboard.

"What's that for?" she asked, noticing the curliness of his short-cut hair.

"My radar detector," he said with pride. "A prototype I developed."

"Why do you need a radar detector?"

"Electronic sensors detect radar signals from as far as a mile away. It sounds an alarm and starts flashing if we pass police radar."

"Like a warning?"

"Precisely. Allows me to drive faster."

For the next fifteen minutes he ignored her. Of course, it wasn't necessary to make conversation. Not everyone needs to talk. He probably had more important things on his mind, like electric circuits. She flipped through *Seventeen* in search of the feature her girlfriends called the "first-kiss" story.

"Prudence," Ivan said. "What kind of a name is that?"

"It's a family name. Mom's ancestor Prudence White arrived on the Mayflower."

She reflected on how lucky she was to have an American mother, parents who didn't force her to speak a foreign language, no extra homework for "Russian" school, and no mandatory church on Sundays.

*

Ivan tapped a rhythm on the steering wheel with his thumb. Prudence hesitated to ask their destination lest he think her rude. She popped a fireball into her mouth. The first suck was the best part, the burning sensation, the jolt of cinnamon. She rolled the candy from one cheek to the other and daydreamed about her transistor radio. It had changed her life, providing not only background music for homework but also constant companionship since her mother didn't come home from work until dinnertime.

She stole a glance at her companion. Ivan seemed pleased with himself, probably because the Rambler was making good time. He had been quiet for so long that his first question caught her off guard, like the meteor she had witnessed that spring: unexpected, fiery, enigmatic: "Do you have a boyfriend?"

Prudence pondered how to respond without telling a lie. "Yes," she said. "Named Ashton. He has another girlfriend, Paige. She lives in Richmond. That's where he lives. But I think he likes me too. Think? Know. He kissed me goodbye last month," she added with an eyeroll to clarify the attraction was mutual, despite recent news from a Richmond friend who reported Paige now wore Ashton's class ring around her neck.

"Ashton, Paige, Prudence. Strange names in this country."

"I can show you his picture if you want, Cousin Ivan."

"That's okay," he said, with a chuckle of condescension.

"It's a shame he likes to play the field. Some boys do."

"What's this *play the field*?"

"More than one girlfriend."

Ivan grappled with the concept for a couple of miles.

"Want to listen to the radio? Be my guest," he said in a friendly tone, giving her the impression that he thought she deserved some sort of consolation prize.

Prudence pressed the buttons until she located a clear signal. She sang along, snapping her fingers in time to the familiar beat. Connie Francis was back on the "Stupid Cupid" refrain about lips of wine when Ivan switched off the radio.

"Hey! You said I could listen."

"That stuff is a waste of time."

Prudence refused to let herself feel disgruntled. Russian fathers didn't get American culture. It was a fact. Her dad had become furious the day he recognized a Bach melody at the beginning of "Beep Beep" by The Playmates, but at least he had allowed her to turn the radio back on afterwards. She suppressed the urge to tell Ivan all teenagers listen to pop music and his kids would too, that he might as well get used to it. They rode on in silence for a while.

"Where are we going anyway?" she asked when he changed lanes and exited the thruway.

"Howe Caverns. Ever been in a cavern?"

Prudence shook her head. "Where will we stay?"

"A motel nearby."

She hadn't brought much money, only twenty dollars. In summer, her family spent a week at a motel in Rehoboth Beach. She shared a room with her brother. What if she had to share a room with Ivan? The thought was unsettling.

*

They sped along, stopping once for gas and a restroom at Howard Johnson's. Prudence hid a yawn as she climbed into the station wagon.

"If you're tired, you can lie down in back. Or you could lay your head against my leg. Makes a nice cushion."

"I'm okay," she said, dismayed at the offer. Could Ivan be attracted to her? As a child, she had napped on her dad's leg on drives through the countryside. The idea of resting her head on Ivan's leg did not appeal to her at all. "Are we almost there?"

"Couple hours more. We'll be on rural roads from now on."

Prudence made a big show of snuggling in against the car door to show she had no intention of using his leg as a cushion.

Although the hill country might have been picturesque during the day, the darkness of night obscured the scenery. White road markers flashed by. Up and down hills they sped. Soon spotlights revealed huge billboards. She dozed off after the two billboards showing happy spelunkers in Howe Caverns and its competitor, Secret Caverns. Ivan swerved up an incline and into a motel parking lot. She opened her eyes in time to see him walk across the lawn and enter an office. The walls of the building were painted lime green.

Here she was, in an unfamiliar place, with no money. What if he went off and left her there? He was such a bizarre fellow. Her parents would be sick with worry if they knew she was alone, in a car, in the middle of nowhere. Five endless minutes ticked by. It was a relief when he reappeared.

"What took so long?" she asked, unable to hide her irritation.

"Those idiots are slow. Like cows."

"I was scared."

Ivan drew a revolver from a concealed body holster. "No need."

Prudence had never met anyone who carried a gun before. She gnawed the inside of her cheek at this development. Fortunately, he didn't pick up on her confusion.

"Why do you wear a gun?"

"Old habit. I was a pilot during the war. Guns became second nature."

"Were you a GI?"

"Not a GI." He replaced the gun in its holster and paused before adding in a lowered voice, "Fought for Germany."

"With the Nazis?"

"Not exactly. I lived in Yugoslavia. But it's a long story. Doubt you'd be interested."

She thought back to geography class with her cute teacher Mr. Hanscomb. "Yugoslavia is near Italy, am I right?"

"Not far away." Ivan shot her an off-kilter smile and dangled in her face a key attached to an orange plastic triangle. "If you encounter problems, bang on the wall."

Separate motel rooms. Side by side, but separate. What a relief.

*

Prudence cracked open the door the next morning and peeked outside. By daylight, the motel was less intimidating. The hot sun reflected white off the corrugated metal roof of the motel office. A man in a straw hat pushed a mower across the lawn. Two boys skipped ahead of their parents, who had stopped beside a wooden sign: *Howe Caverns, Gift Shop and Restaurant, Elevation 1063', Straight Ahead.* There was a breakfast tray on the doormat: a box of Rice Krispies, a package of Twinkies, an orange, a carton of milk. From the accompanying note—*Off on business, back soon*—she gathered Ivan had gone to meet someone connected with his job. They were probably busy talking electronic gadgets. She knew business deals required face-to-face negotiation. But he could have mentioned the appointment. What a jerk.

She took her time getting dressed. Bermuda shorts and Mila's blouse would have to do. While dressing, she inspected the sorry motel room with its clunky RCA television. Cigarette burns on the carpet. Pistachio-colored walls. Leaky bathroom faucet. At least there was an air-conditioner. It heaved a heavy sigh as she pushed ON.

The Rambler swerved into the parking lot two hours later. Ivan had exchanged his loafers for sneakers, which made the rumpled gray suit look even more ridiculous. He handed her a bag of tuna sandwiches. Had he met a fellow research scientist? Her best friend's elder brother attended Cornell. No doubt Ivan had spent the morning in Ithaca. She would have liked details. In a similar situation, her mom would have plied him with questions, so Prudence inquired whether he had been able to close the deal.

The question made him laugh. "Looks like it. I'd say I closed the deal."

They joined the tourists heading toward a one-story building at the top of the hill. Three-quarters of the way up, Ivan suggested lunch. Several picnic tables overlooked a grassy meadow. The sky was cobalt blue. Puffy white clouds rode across the horizon.

"A farmer discovered this place," he said, eating his tuna sandwich with less haste than usual. "His cows preferred a certain part of the pasture, where it was cooler, because of the caverns below."

"Cows?"

"As in moo-ooo." It wasn't a bad imitation, which made her relax somehow. Maybe her cousin was a regular guy after all, not simply a disciplinarian spaz.

"Can you do that again, Cousin Ivan?"

"Moo-ooo," he repeated. "And stop this 'Cousin Ivan' business. Call me Ivan."

"You're funny," she said, observing him with more attention.

Ivan crushed the sandwich wrapper. He took his time and seemed absorbed in the noise made by the crinkly cellophane. She stood up then, brushing crumbs off her new blouse. He placed his hands on her shoulders and spun her body around, the way he had done with his daughters on the rare good-mood day. Breaking free, she set off at a trot.

Ivan strode into the gift shop to purchase tickets. Prudence circled the postcard racks. Nearby, on a counter, shiny rocks were for sale. She slipped a 99-cent hunk of quartz into her pocket for Roksana, the first time she had ever stolen anything. It felt exhilarating. Back outside, Ivan motioned her into line and removed his tie, jamming it into a back pocket. Twin girls, not much older than Niko, jumped up and down in front of an elevator built into the rock face. They squealed with excitement while their mother fastened the buttons on identical sweaters. Prudence fanned herself with a Howe Caverns brochure. Someone had dropped an ice cream sandwich near the elevator. She watched ants wade through the melted ice cream and wondered what people did underground if seized by claustrophobia.

The elevator door sprang open to release several dozen tourists. A red light flashed green. Prudence waited on a family who took their time, boisterous in Cincinnati Reds regalia. The tour guide yanked the accordion gate, which rolled into place with a metallic rattle. Her stomach tightened during the descent. Hoist cables jingle-jangled all the way down. Beads of sweat dotted her brow by the time the elevator jerked to a stop.

The guide stepped onto a platform, protected from the pitch-black cavern by a guardrail, and called out, "Greetings, future spelunkers. My name's Clarence. We are now one hundred and fifty-six feet below the earth's surface." His voice reverberated off the walls. "Hope you folks brought sweaters. The temperature down here is fifty-two degrees."

It was cold and damp and dark as a moonless night. Prudence gave an involuntary shudder as the other members of the group moved toward a cement staircase, their progress hindered by the slippery brick walkway and the occasional splash from a stream that rushed past the elevator shaft. When she lifted her eyes in search of the ceiling, water dripped onto her face, random droplets that assaulted the skin like pinpricks.

"Follow me," Ivan said. "Last spring you said you were up for anything."

"I do love adventure, but this place gives me the creeps."

The tourists funneled down additional steps, more treacherous and slightly curved. Was it the change in pressure that made her nervous or the risk of entrapment? What if their guide suffered a heart attack? How would they escape? "Accepting Ivan's invitation to go underground was such a bad idea," she muttered as they hurried along.

Florescent lights illuminated The Pipe Organ. Prudence giant-stepped away from the abyss, one hand curled tight around the guardrail. Slimy wetness coated what a brass plaque identified as flowstone. She did her best to appreciate the mass of stalagmites and stalactites that had fused together. Nope. F minus. A career as a spelunker was not in her future. Her teeth chattered from the cold. That was when Ivan removed his jacket and draped it over her shoulders.

"Thanks. What about you?"

"I'm warm-blooded." He smiled in a new way, patronizing but chummy, as if the two of them had shared a marvelous private joke.

The tour group filed into Titan's Temple, a vast chamber with vaulted ceiling. The dank atmosphere became more oppressive. At the Bridal Altar, the irregular brickwork made Prudence stumble. Ivan caught her fall.

"Don't miss these walls," he said. "Limestone. The black smudges are from torches in the 1840s."

Smudge marks? She gave her shoulders a roll and hugged herself, clasping the rickrack on Mila's blouse. She couldn't care less about smudge marks.

Clarence blew his whistle. He had stopped beside a body of brackish water to describe the rock formations through a bullhorn. The tourists fell silent.

"Holy moly! What's that?"

"A lake," Ivan replied, implying the climax of the guided tour was a feature to remember all one's life. He rubbed his hands together. She couldn't tell whether it was from enthusiasm or a need to stay warm.

"I don't want to go for a ride on an underground lake."

Apparently, the twins' mother shared her apprehension because Clarence lifted the bullhorn to his mouth. "The Lake of Venus is only two to six feet deep. No need for alarm, folks. In case of emergency, our team has life-saving credentials."

Prudence climbed into one of two shallow boats, followed by the family from Cincinnati. Ivan sat down beside her, so close she could feel his body heat. She would have liked more space, but the narrow seats made that impossible.

"We'll go to the waterfall and back," Clarence intoned. "That's when things can get scary. Why? We briefly extinguish the lights. All you parents, grab your kids' hands. Everybody ready? Off we go!"

The boat glided through the murky darkness. In its wake, ripples formed on the glassy surface. From the steady forward motion, she understood that the hull was attached to a cable, which assuaged her anxiety. Funny how this underground world followed its own set of rules. An artificial body of water, a rudderless boat that steered itself, deep darkness allowing a man to sit practically on top of you without fear of rebuke.

The waterfall turned out to be a piddling stream that cascaded from above, a much less impressive sight than what was depicted on the gift shop postcards. The lights went out, and the boat reversed course.

At first, it didn't seem strange to have Ivan place his hand on hers. Her dad might have acted in a similar manner to ease her discomfort. But Ivan closed his palm over her fingers and squeezed. Prudence froze, realizing this was not an innocent pat. She tried to remove the hand without being too obvious about it, but he tightened his grip, and her heart raced. Her instinct had been right. He was attracted to her. This unlikely premise grew more credible with each new rock formation that lurched into view.

*

When Ivan strode ahead on the sidewalk leading back to the motel, Prudence wondered whether she had imagined it all: the body heat, the pressure of his hand, the subtle change in attitude. She had assumed he might go for a kiss and felt sorry to learn he needed to make a few phone calls. Not what she had expected but that was fine. No, better, really. Kissing Mila's husband wouldn't be proper. All the same, it would have been a fun experience to be kissed goodnight by a man twice her age.

A feather in her cap as far as girlfriends were concerned. Most of them could only claim Spin-the-Bottle kisses and admired anyone who had been kissed by more than one boy. Her mom tried to prevent her from kissing Ashton. When they made out in the basement rec-room, they'd hear noise from the kitchen above: the banging of pots and pans, the buzzing of her brother's kazoo, phone calls supposedly from girlfriends who hung up by the time she climbed the basement steps.

Ivan knocked on the door an hour later and escorted her to dinner. Buck Owens' "Act Naturally" played on the jukebox in the cozy Howe Caverns restaurant with its wood-paneled walls and colorful promotional photos in plastic frames painted gold. The dining room smelled of spearmint gum. She felt grown up, seated in a booth beside a cousin her parents held in high esteem. Ivan ordered the house special for them both: meatloaf, green peas, mashed potatoes.

"What would you like to drink?"

Prudence ran her finger down the menu options and chose Coke, curious whether he would object since his kids were not allowed to drink the sugary beverage. Ivan said not a word. This lack of censure loosened her tongue.

"Can you tell me about flying planes for Germany?" she asked.

"They were Messerschmitts Bf 109s."

"Did they carry bombs?"

"It was war, so yes. You know, I'd prefer we talk about something else."

Prudence had no problem with this request. She told him how grateful she was for transistors. She listed her top ten songs, all Motown except for the Everly Brothers, and described a typical day at Roland Park Middle School. She said her best subjects were Latin and Geography and would he like her to name the countries of Europe and guess which ones he had visited? Ivan, who had finished his meal, said he wasn't interested in European countries, so she moved on to her best friend Sarah Hawkins and explained how they had crawled out Sarah's window onto a shingled overhang, warmed by the setting sun, and searched the night sky for shooting stars to celebrate summer vacation.

Ivan laughed at the shooting stars story and made a remark about giving Roksana a whipping should she try a similar prank. "My daughters would never get away with that," he added under his breath.

After the meal, they walked back down the hill. Only the low hum of crickets broke the silence. During their absence, cars had filled the parking lot.

As they approached the motel door, Prudence was describing how different her life would be that fall because of attending a new school. "They make us wear these ugly uniforms. It's a requirement." She paused to fiddle with the key. To her embarrassment, Ivan took it out of her hand and unlocked the door. The manager turned on the No Vacancy sign, which flashed red. Standing there in the garish glow of the porch light reminded her of the July issue of *Seventeen*, where the science teacher kissed the prom queen goodnight.

"Thank you for a nice evening," Ivan said. He folded his glasses into a breast pocket and, in no time, had slipped his arm around her waist. "Were you aware of what a successful career your grandfather had in the military? Too bad he snubbed the Moscow cousins. Wouldn't agree to meet with my uncles."

"How could you have known my grandfather?" she said, aghast. "You're not that old, are you?" This was his first mention of family and distant family at that.

"The general was a legend for my generation. What would he have thought of us together?" Ivan gave her that proprietary smile again as if she were one of his patents, ready for presentation to competitors.

Prudence said nothing, wondering how to disengage.

"There's an expression I learned in your country."

"What's that?"

"Kissing cousins. Heard of it?"

There was such intensity in his dark eyes.

She never paid attention when her dad discussed Russia and had no idea what Ivan meant when he said her grandfather had snubbed his uncles. And now he had used a colloquial expression with an obscure meaning, and she wasn't sure how to respond.

"Sounds silly, like something Ashton would invent."

"Prudence, you told me Ashton kissed you."

"Ye-es," she replied. He stood so close she could smell his breath. She had two choices. Ask him to step away or step away herself.

"Are you a virgin?"

His head bobbed toward hers. Their lips touched. The kiss went on and on. The experience turned out to be more pleasant than she could have anticipated, better, in fact, than kissing Ashton.

With a measure of unease, Prudence realized she wanted him to kiss her again. They had already broken the rules. What difference would another kiss make?

Ivan pushed open the door with his foot. The air-conditioning unit kicked in. Down at the end of the motel, someone raised the volume on a TV. She switched on the overhead light. He switched it off again. Timidly, she reached out to fondle his hair.

"You women are all the same," he said with a chuckle.

"What about your wife?" she whispered.

"Mila knows I love her. Nothing wrong with a bit of . . . what do you Americans call it?" He stroked her cheek. "Hanky-panky?"

*

Back in Connecticut the next day, Prudence joined Mila on the sun porch. Mila's fingers effortlessly worked a crochet hook in and out of what resembled a baby bootie. Stitches appeared, one after the other, symmetrical and neat. Prudence felt like someone had branded an A on her forehead. Did she look different? Smell different? What was wrong with lying naked, beside a man in boxers? She hadn't let him get much past second base. No harm in a few stolen kisses, he had said before they parted company in front of the white Colonial. A smile slid across her face at the memory.

His wife deserved better. Stoic, genteel, patient, wise, generous, open-minded, non-judgmental—complimentary adjectives kept popping into her head. She felt a surge of gratitude for the mature woman by her side who had provided pads and a belt for her period, which had come early.

On the drive home, in fact. Menstruation would require adjustment.

Mila finished the bootie. "Okay," she said. "Now, we need to talk."

Prudence hardly dared to breathe, her heart seizing up. "Talk about what? What do we need to talk about?"

In the yard, Niko swung at the air with Roksana's butterfly net. His sisters had left to play hula-hoop with the kids next door. From the kitchen came the sharp whistle of the Revere Ware kettle.

"Ivan said you're to wear a uniform at school. I wore one in France. Why don't you pick out an A-line dress? They're easy to sew. If you run into any trouble, I'll be glad to give advice over the phone."

"You don't have to do that."

"Oh, but I want to." Mila extended her hand to indicate the Simplicity catalog on the floor. "Can you give me the Simplicity pattern book please?"

Prudence did as Mila requested.

"You're becoming a woman now. You'll be able to dress up for the weekend. Why not choose a pattern?"

There was no malice in Mila's voice, although she did peer over at her guest before retreating into the kitchen to prepare afternoon tea.

Prudence felt relieved to have escaped confrontation. Her mind replayed what had happened at the motel. She stared down at her bare feet, wriggled her toes, moved the fireball in her mouth to the other cheek. No one had called her a woman before. She liked the power of it and was filled with a delicious sense of life's possibilities.

The Revelation

In the middle of October, the Menshikovs invited us to a luncheon. Lizzie and I had been married for eight months by then. Our baby was due in January. On the drive into Paris, I joked about filling in for VIPs. Important people often cancel at the last minute. Lizzie had come to call on the prince during a previous trip to France, bearing a letter of introduction from her father. The two men had lived on the same street in Leningrad before the Russian Revolution and followed each other's careers in their respective countries through brief notes scribbled on Christmas cards.

Lizzie thought the world of Maxim Menshikov.

They met again, after her aunt's death. The mailing address near Trocadero had led Lizzie to believe Tania owned a high-end apartment, worthy of a woman known to have inspired Europe's most celebrated photographers. The visit obliged her to abandon her notions of old-world privilege and accept the fact that Tania had climbed five flights of stairs to access a former maid's room, eight feet by ten, with a communal toilet and shower. As I helped my sensitive wife carry a pile of 78-RPMs from our car, she went on and on about the sparse furnishings, the two-inch mattress on the iron bedframe, the faded wallpaper, the photo of Valentino tucked into a brace on the mirror.

"I'd feel better if I knew she had been able to listen to Maurice Chevalier," Lizzie said, pursing her lips as she paused to read a record label. "Might have provided comfort."

"No record player?"

"Sold, no doubt, to pay the bills." She frowned. "Prince Menshikov has money. Why not hire movers?"

"Maybe he wanted you to grasp how fleeting glory can be?"

"No. There's more to it. You should have seen him, seated there on the bed, sifting through packets of correspondence. When he thought I wasn't looking, he'd slip letters into his pocket. Now, why would he do that?"

Lizzie added that Menshikov had mentioned he hoped to meet her *intriguing French husband* (me!) and would have us over as soon as his schedule allowed. That opportunity had come at last.

Traffic thinned out at the Porte de St. Cloud. Aiming to arrive by 12:30, I sped up Boulevard Exelmans. I hated being late. We ran traffic lights. Three of them. Lizzie's mind was back on her poor aunt.

"Did I tell you Tania's ex married an heiress from Connecticut? The guy founded an association to help White Russians. He paid her rent, so I guess the prince acted as a go-between and—" Lizzie stopped speaking, her eyes on a billboard. "Oh, Adam, look! It's Michel Polnareff. He has no pants on."

I had heard about the comeback concert at Olympia but not the promotional campaign. A floppy sunhat covered the signature blond curls. A sprig of artificial cherries decorated his only garment, ruffled and white. Polnareff wore sunglasses, white-framed and rectangular. The singer peered over his shoulder in a provocative way.

Lizzie kept staring at the image as we drove past.

"Nice ass," I said with a wink.

"Well, he shouldn't show it off in public," she huffed, opening the glove compartment for her atomizer. "He may sing like an angel, but what has gotten into the man, posing half naked?"

"Love me," I sang. "Please love me." I may have sung the first line of his latest hit with more of an accent than the singer, but, on the second line, I clearly outdid him, letting my voice quiver in falsetto, "Je suis fou de v-o-oo-ous."

Lizzie broke into that knockout smile of hers.

We were lucky to find a parking space right off the Rue de la Tour. From my pocket came a tin of breath mints. I checked my appearance in the sun visor mirror—wide executive necktie, nicely trimmed sideburns—and stepped out of the car.

Lizzie sprayed Jean Naté onto her wrist, tightened her ponytail, and raised her chin. "How do I look?"

"Besides pregnant? Lovely, as ever."

My wife did look amazing, her cheeks as rosy as the see-through fabric of her raspberry-colored blouse. A salesgirl had convinced us that it complimented the pricey maternity outfit, a sleeveless blue wool tunic with matching flared trousers.

In my jacket pocket, a paisley square matching the weave of my new business suit. I'd paid extra attention to my wardrobe ever since Lizzie described her former boyfriend as a snappy dresser. I could barely believe she had chosen to marry me when she could have waited for Reggie to finish law school. Reginald Beauregard Lee was a direct descendant of the Confederate general and a handsome one at that. Lizzie's ancestors were military men who led armies and owned castles. Mine built cobblestone roads in Burgundy. We socialized in cafés. Although I was a graduate of the prestigious École des Mines, I worried that she might feel ashamed of my background, that our child might chaff at the limitations imposed by class.

I was filled with excitement at the idea of meeting a real prince. We didn't have any princes in Dijon, only mustard kings. My father-in-law's friend was royalty of some kind, affluent, influential. Now that our meeting was imminent, my pulse quickened, and the tin of breath mints slipped from my moist hand.

"Dad's friend is like a walking Rolodex," Lizzie said at the lacquered exterior door. "He knows all the important people in the White Russian community. I wouldn't be surprised if he has met Polnareff."

The building reminded me of my cousins' apartment in the tenth arrondissement, my home away from home while at university, except the décor was classier than any fourth-floor walk-up. Case in point, the private elevator. Up we went to the fifth floor.

Prince Menshikov squeezed the elevator cage gate open and greeted us with gusto: kisses for Lizzie, a buoyant hug for me. He wore a pinstriped three-piece suit with a silk scarf tucked into the breast pocket and the red rosette of the Legion of Honor at the lapel. His movements were swift, his gaze piercing. Although his double chin spoke of a life of luxury, he was in remarkably good shape for a sixty-five-year-old businessman.

"Call me Galina, yes?" Princess Menshikov said. "You are ze newlyweds. You sit *ensemble* at ze table? Geeve me jacket, Adam."

I was happy to oblige, intent on making a good impression.

Galina's shapeless beige gown matched the brocade drapes drawn across the entrance door. Her limpid brown eyes were slightly crossed, her nose sharp and pointed, her wispy hair collected into a neat bun, which gave her the air of a startled ostrich. She led us into the dining room. Its north-facing wall featured a leaded-glass window, Art Deco in style: purple wisteria blossoms twined with lime-green leaves. Instead of fried mackerel or slow-cooked beef, the air smelled faintly of lilac talcum powder and bergamot. The immaculate mahogany sideboard, the heavy linen tablecloth, and the silver bowl of white carnations made the place feel more like a social club than a private home.

Prince Menshikov had decanted a bottle of Château de Beaucastel Châteauneuf-du-Pape, 1970. Now, he uncorked celebratory champagne and filled our flutes with a flourish. Lizzie, who didn't drink because of her pregnancy, accepted a half-glass of bubbly while I was on my knees, fiddling with the call button at Galina's request.

We all sat down at the highly polished oval table, and a maid carried in the first course: *Moules Marinières*.

"How do you like Paris?" our host asked. "Has it lived up to your expectations?"

"Totally," Lizzie said. "I especially love the smell in the Métro."

Galina flipped open her fan. The crystal teardrops on her vintage bracelet click-clicked as she held the fan to her heavily powdered face.

"The Métro?" Menshikov repeated with some disbelief. "Wouldn't know, my dear. My chauffeur drives us around these days."

The prince used an opened mussel shell as a pincer to extract the meat. I followed his lead.

"On the way over, we saw the most incredible thing," Lizzie continued.

Time for our secret signal that a subject is inappropriate. I raised my voice. "Are you referring to President Pompidou's motorcade?"

"What did you see, my dear?" Galina asked.

"You know Michel Polnareff, the singer?" Lizzie replied, giving me the evil eye. "We saw an advertisement for his comeback concert. Polnareff wasn't wearing any pants."

"I've heard the lad likes to behave in a manner most of us would consider outré," Menshikov said.

"So, you do know him?" Lizzie asked exuberantly.

"Not exactly." He turned his head and held my gaze. "I knew his dad who used to write songs for Piaf."

Under the table, my knee bounced up and down. None of this advanced my goal. What I craved was an opportunity to mention my recent promotion at Schlumberger. The firm had a solid reputation. The prince could only be impressed.

Lizzie grinned at me as the maid carried in a dish she had never attempted: *Pigeon aux Petits Pois,* my mother's specialty. The little squares of bacon were tasty; the garnish of oven-roasted fingerling potatoes, crisp.

I missed whole swaths of conversation since Galina spoke English with an accent. The two women discussed our baby's future religion—not Orthodox, to Galina's dismay—the first names we had chosen, and the items that remained on our baby list at Le Printemps. Prince Menshikov kept glancing at his Rolex. I couldn't help but wonder why he had summoned Lizzie if he was eager to have us leave.

I felt more at ease by the time the maid brought dessert, gossamer-light meringues floating in a pool of vanilla custard.

"Do you enjoy ballet?" Menshikov asked. "The Kirov is in town. A trip abroad will make me miss the performance. Would you like our tickets?"

Early-to-bed, early-to-rise, Lizzie declined.

Menshikov proceeded to talk ballet, praising Nureyev, whom he had met at a charity ball.

Either preoccupied or bored to tears, Galina fiddled with a dessert fork and didn't make eye contact. "Nureyev again," she muttered, helping herself to more wine.

"Prince Menshikov, please do tell us about your work," Lizzie said.

"Moët & Chandon has purchased Christian Dior, but I doubt my work would interest you."

Galina removed a cigarette from an enameled case. I sparked my Zippo, hoping her husband would say more. How he had gotten the job, what position he held, whether working for the fashion house involved any travel. After lighting my own Gitane, I blew three perfect smoke rings over my shoulder, toward the retreating servant, who had produced two balloon snifters and a bottle of Rémy Martin.

The prince raised his glass in my direction as if to imply we shared an appreciation for the finer things in life. To my surprise, he leaned forward and whispered, "We are alike in more ways than you may realize."

I gave a stiff little nod, unsure what he meant but not inclined to take issue with it. Galina grimaced, sucking on her cigarette. As the luncheon concluded, the room fell silent. From the kitchen came the rattle of plates. The two-tone siren of a police car drifted up from the street. I was about to broach the subject of my job search when our hosts spoke at once. They both stopped mid-sentence.

"You go, Max," Galina said, eyes on the ceiling.

"No. You dear. What were you about to say?"

Galina asked Lizzie to join her in the bedroom, a request that made the skin around her eyes crinkle in a kindly way.

Menshikov offered up a furtive scowl, apologetic, somewhat contrite. "Yes," he agreed. "It's time. Let's adjourn with our Cognac."

I trailed the ladies into the drawing room, where Galina opened a bedroom door. I glimpsed a mirrored dressing table with a gathered skirt of eyelet fabric and candy-striped wallpaper. Lizzie threw me her who-knows-what's-up look. The padded door closed with a soft thud. I stood in front of a Florentine wall mirror, studying its swirls.

The prince, who had ducked into the kitchen after the meal, snapped his fingers to indicate I should follow. He cradled a rather large Chinese vase. "Picked this up in Shanghai," he said, although I had not asked. "There's a hairline crack, which is why I need it to go in my den from now on. This way."

I could understand how the princess might have squirreled away a present for our baby in her private quarters—a romper suit or an anklet fashioned out of gold—but an invitation from her husband to explore a whole other wing of the vast apartment felt most out of the ordinary.

Menshikov led the way down a dark hall into a bedroom, its walls upholstered in claret-colored velvet. I trailed him into the adjoining den. He had me sit in one of two overstuffed leather armchairs beside an ornate Louis XIV kneehole desk, and, wasting no time, went straight to the point: "I received a phone call yesterday from Lizzie's parents. I regret to inform you that her former boyfriend in Manhattan has committed suicide."

"Suicide!" I exclaimed, letting my mouth hang open while the news sank in. As I juggled the paltry details Lizzie had provided, my thoughts zeroed in on whether the shock might affect our unborn child, which also seemed to be the prince's primary concern.

"Does she know?"

"Good God, no. We had no idea."

"That's what we assumed. Hence the urgency of this visit. Due to her delicate condition, Yuri and Carolyn would prefer to have you inform their daughter of his demise. And offer comfort, of course. Care for a cigar?" When I shook my head, he lit up, studying my face over his gold-rimmed spectacles.

Here was the reason for the precipitous invitation. My father-in-law had asked the prince to serve as messenger.

"How?" I managed, raising my eyebrows.

"Jumped out a window."

He slit open several bills with a silver paper knife. It was good of him to drop his eyes. I preferred to keep my emotions to myself. I was remembering the day Lizzie told me about a Dear John letter, mailed from Paris to New York after we started dating, my first inkling of the existence of a steady boyfriend. They were to travel around Europe together, a plan our meeting disrupted. It was impossible not to feel a certain amount of guilt since Lizzie had left him to marry me. Could he have killed himself on my account? I shuddered at the thought. Poor Reggie. I had assumed he had been able to move on with his life.

The prince puffed away on his cigar, enjoying every minute of the smoke. "Galina doesn't allow these beauties in the apartment," he said in response to my inquisitive stare.

"Of course," I muttered, addled by my new knowledge.

"I suggest you start by saying there's been an accident." He stroked the triangular scar on his chin, then aimed his cigar at a marble clock on the mantelpiece. "I suppose we should be getting back."

An accident, destroying oneself. Start there and observe Lizzie's reaction. Easy enough. Grimly, I rose to my feet.

The prince extinguished his cigar in a standing ashtray and pushed the filigreed cover into place. He extended his arm. "After you."

We crossed the bedroom to the hallway and were about to enter the drawing room. My mind was on events of the previous summer, the suicide, suitable phrasing for the revelation entrusted to me, when Menshikov pinched my butt cheek. Before I could react, he swung open the door, and we faced the ladies, seated on the couch. For a split second I felt embarrassed by my reflection in the mirror, eyes wider than usual, nose out of joint, but Lizzie didn't notice.

"Galina has given me a bracelet that belonged to Aunt Tania," she said, her pretty face aglow. "Isn't it gorgeous?"

The sapphires sparkled as she twirled her hand. Galina clapped, setting the crystal teardrops on her plump wrist to clicking. The prince picked up a globular silver-gilt lighter from the coffee table and rotated it several times, presumably unwilling to pay us any more attention.

The playful pinch was an entirely unnerving experience. Did he think I was a homosexual? Lizzie had always praised the prince as a model of decorum. Pinching me. Good God. What had gotten into the man?

At least the luncheon went well. I left with more confidence in myself, no longer afraid that my humble origins might negatively impact our baby's future.

I put off telling Lizzie the unfortunate news about Reggie until the weekend. She attributed the suicide to his service in Vietnam and cried but for less time than I expected. We discussed a letter of condolence to the parents. She settled on a note to his sister. I could only conclude Reggie had not mattered all that much, although her smile wasn't as bright for weeks.

I struggled to find the right moment to mention the pinch.

"That doesn't sound possible," Lizzie said, hand clasped to her mouth.

"I've heard homosexuals are discreet."

"Remember me telling you about those letters in Tania's trunk? No doubt they contained details about some secret affair."

We dropped the subject, swept up with preparation for Tatiana's birth.

The following week I answered a classified ad Lizzie spotted in *L'Express*. My new HR job at Air France included free travel for family members as part of the benefits package. I started work at Orly on December 1.

Seven days later a judge fined Polnareff 60,000 francs and reprimanded the singer for indecency.

While Lizzie was at the American Hospital, Galina and
Maxim Menshikov sent over a gold gourmet bracelet and a
bouquet of pink peonies. I didn't change my opinion of the
prince, an upright citizen who, Lizzie maintained, had done
much to help the White Russian community. What I do know
is that he never invited us to lunch again.

Buried Treasure

I kneel beside a bag of mulch, digging with a trowel between two stone-encased flowerbeds, when the thought of our future holiday in Russia makes me hum "Vacation" by the Go-Gos. I added the trip to my bucket list after Aunt Maria's funeral. I'm hoping to visit the graves of my great grandparents. My husband wants to see the tattooed man in the Hermitage Museum. Erik teaches history at the Swedish School of London. Once he's home from work, we'll talk more about the eventual recovery of real estate that belonged to my family before the Russian Revolution and establish a list of priorities for our weekend in St. Petersburg. I clear away a layer of dead leaves before scratching lines in the hard-packed earth. It would be brilliant to discover an ancient Roman mosaic under the abandoned flowerbeds. The final step is to slip in a shovel and lift away dirt. But wait. What's this? I scrape some more and unearth a soil-encrusted ball. I rub off the dirt. I've found a marble. Orange swirls through the gorgeous green.

*

Two weeks later, Erik and I fly to Stockholm. After a night in the city, we take a train north to Arlanda Airport. I strap my violin case to my back and off we go via elevator, following the yellow Departures signs. At the turnstile, Erik meets his son Martin, a second-year university student in Uppsala. The two men greet each other with a great slapping of arms and chuckles of endearment while I jot a few words on a postcard for my parents in San Francisco.

On our walk to the gate, we stop at a kiosk, where I purchase a bag of Daim chocolates, three oranges, and the most recent James Bond. Erik picks up the latest issue of Newsweek. As I search my purse for Aunt Maria's treasure map, I trip over a metal bar between the tiled walkway and the SAS passenger lounge. Everything in my arms goes flying: Lonely Planet guidebook, fruit, *Death is Forever*.

A man in a pale-yellow suit powers past, wheeling a suitcase, sleek and sturdy like its owner. We follow the stranger to a row of connected seats and sit down nearby. The man has high cheekbones, a dark complexion, and coarse black hair drawn into a neat ponytail. Even more striking is his three-piece suit, custom-made by an Armani wannabe. How extraordinary the color, like egg yolk beaten with sugar. The suit hints at privilege and a certain ruthlessness required to achieve high social rank in modern Russia. I watch as he excavates a narrow box from a shopping bag. Head down, he takes his time opening the box and fastening the clasp on a gold watch. With a grunt of satisfaction, he extends his wrist and mutters what must be words of gratitude to the Gods of Patronage who allow such toys.

"Ten to one he's a Mafioso," I say under my breath.

"Today's robber barons," Erik replies as he flips through Newsweek.

*

During the flight, Martin informs his father that he plans to switch from classics to computer science, a field with greater job opportunity. I half-listen, busy twisting open the Matryoshka doll that is our visit to St. Petersburg. Nestled inside lurks the possibility of reclaiming my father's childhood home near the Summer Garden. For years, I've allowed myself to dream of renovation, but the project never seemed realistic, even after glasnost loosened governmental control. Now, in my mind, painters and plasterers and carpenters hammer away in a futile effort to return the thirty rooms to their former glory.

At Pulkovo Airport, the customs official eyes my round face as if he has some detention quota to fill and stamps my passport with mild disapproval, circling the visa expiration date, September 25, 1997. Relieved that no one has opened our hand luggage or my violin case, I rush to catch up with the two Swedes.

"It's incredible to be this close to Stockholm and know that one million people starved to death here," Erik says with a gesture toward the southern horizon. "The Nazis occupied those hills. Long-range artillery fire."

Our taxi speeds past apartment blocks, row after row of five-story concrete buildings. Urban sprawl has changed the city my father loved. During the Siege of Leningrad, its citizens resorted to eating bark according to National Geographic. I stare out the window at the women clad in nondescript gray or black, colorful kerchiefs on their heads, heavyset women whose underarms probably smell of hard labor.

Hotel Moscow is convenient to the Alexander Nevsky Monastery but lacks glamour. At least key access cards open hotel room doors. On our way back to the lobby, I try out a straight-backed chair, tight against the faded wallpaper, and imagine a plump dowager seated there to record the comings and goings of foreign guests—the *dezhurnaia* of my spy novels.

First order of business: finding Dad's childhood home. We set off through the unfamiliar streets although the sky is overcast, not ideal weather for sight-seeing. Past shops, restaurants, and a nail salon we go. Thirty minutes later, I draw in a sharp breath at seeing our family crest carved into the stone portal of a pink neo-classical building. Dad was born on the fourth floor. It was his whole world until age fifteen.

Martin explores an adjoining passageway and waves at us to join him. We find ourselves in an inner courtyard, rife with the stench of urine. I sink onto a concrete bench and let my eyes play over our surroundings. They deviate from the airbrushed images of my dreams. Walls blackened by soot. Hard-packed cement dust underfoot. Faded blue paint peeling off a dilapidated basement door. I focus in on the bay window that juts out from the fourth floor. The bulge corresponds to my grandparents' ballroom, which featured prominently in the bedtime stories Dad told in lieu of fairy tales. For eighty years strangers have lived here, strangers like the close-lipped pedestrians who file past on the street. Are they descendants of revolutionaries or victims of revolution?

"I can't help but wonder what life was like under Communism," I murmur and clasp my breast, eyes welling up at the upheaval caused by massive emigration and civil war.

Erik packs a wad of chewing tobacco under his lip. His eyes narrow from the nicotine surge. "Oh, there were huge benefits for the common people. Years ago, I took a sauna with an anarchist who volunteered to fight with the Bolsheviks. He met

Stalin. He met Lenin. I asked whether he felt disappointed in the outcome."

Martin dribbles an empty vodka bottle across the courtyard. "And what did the guy say?"

"Revolution was the first time the working class came to power. The whole idea gave Russians hope."

"Martin, did you know the new regime called aristocrats 'former people?'" Doing my best to disregard Erik's admiration for the Communists who control my father's homeland, I continue, "Dad's apartment was divvied up to accommodate a number of families, like in *Dr. Zhivago.*"

"Appropriated?"

"Stolen. Purloined. Impounded."

Our conversation amuses Erik. "Should we try to go upstairs?" he asks with a wink.

"Knock on doors? Say, oh hi. My family owned this building before the Bolsheviks kicked them out."

"If you decide to stake a claim, it would be advantageous to know what state the flat is in first."

Was he being facetious? I hate it when he uses that tone of voice, cloying, sardonic, not supportive at all. He made it sound like my ancestors were ogres, rich landowners who oppressed the lower classes.

"I've told you. I don't intend to *stake a claim.*"

Any claim of ownership would involve lawyers, paperwork, migraines. My parents keep the deed in a steamer trunk. On my trip to California in 1995, I went up into the attic and verified its existence, running fingers across the red wax seal. The trunk holds memories dating back years: black and white photographs of family members dressed in gowns with tight bodices and leg-of-mutton sleeves, a cardboard box containing military service medals, ribbons, and other imperial decorations, Dad's old Nansen passport, a four-leaf clover that didn't bring much luck but has been preserved in waxed paper all the same.

*

We visit the Fortress of Peter and Paul. We admire the statue of Peter the Great, tour the Kazan Cathedral. We attend a concert in an ornate theater that has been the center of the city's musical life for 150 years. Our sightseeing frenzy culminates in the Hermitage Museum basement, where we gawk at the upper arm of a Pazyryk chieftain, dating from the fifth century BC. Two vintage spotlights illuminate the display case. Erik leans in to inspect the yellowed skin. The ghoulish artifact shows interlocking beasts, deer with elongated antlers, mountain goats, leaping horses.

"Nice tattoos," Martin said, stroking his buzz-cut hair.

I marvel at the bluish-gray designs. They date from long ago but seem contemporary, like custom body art available at some upscale studio.

"Discovered by Soviet archeologist Sergei Rudenko, who excavated Iron Age tombs in the forties. Barrow-like tomb mounds, not unlike in Uppsala," Eric tells us.

I hug myself, spooked by the dark recesses of the museum basement. "Dear Lord," I say with a shiver. "Don't they have a budget for electrical upgrades?"

"He was buried with a Caucasian woman," Erik adds. "This man once had high prestige."

"*Sic transit Gloria mundi*," Martin calls from the marble staircase.

"Something about how glory is fleeting?"

"Dearest, you took the words right out of my mouth," Erik says.

*

Later that day, we enter the grounds of the Alexander Nevsky Monastery, a Lonely Planet "top choice." I bring my umbrella and strap on my violin case. Erik and Martin wear their raincoats. It begins to drizzle as we pay the admission fee. The air is raw. Mist hovers over trees. After a few false turns, we locate a marker fashioned out of shiny black marble, impervious to the weather. Cyrillic lettering provides an explanation of the cemetery layout. To our chagrin, no one bothered to translate.

Erik has been reading the guidebook. He tucks it under his arm. "This is, and I quote, *where visitors pay their respects to the most illustrious individuals in Russian music, literature, art and theatre.*"

With extreme care, I withdraw from my pocket the treasure map, tattered at the edges. "We're hunting for a brick mausoleum." I lower my voice. "Before she died, Aunt Maria told me her mom buried a jewelry box there before they fled south."

"Did she say what was inside?" asks Martin.

"A ruby tiara. We'll dig it up."

Erik cocks a finger at me "You, my dear, are going to get us into trouble."

"Rubbish." I hand him my umbrella before unfolding the map.

Martin moves in for a closer look. "Super cool."

"Aunt Maria must have carried this throughout her travels."

"How did she manage to leave Russia?"

"They were in Crimea. She took a steamer to Constantinople. Modern-day Istanbul. She lived in Paris, Tokyo, Shanghai, San Francisco, London."

"Did she say where we should search?"

"Near . . . Tchaikovsky."

But we have gone in the wrong direction and find ourselves in a part of the cemetery abandoned to time. The graves are jammed together. Wrought-iron railings surround individual plots. Crosses hang here and there, askew or knocked off pedestals. Tree trunks push through cracks in tombstones, dislodging slabs of granite. I feel like we have entered a house of mirrors, and each curved surface only reflects additional horror. A deep sense of sadness overwhelms me at the evidence of neglect. No one has cleared away the weeds. No one has brought floral sprays or a sprig of wildflowers. I dig my nails into my palms, unsure about owning property in a country with such obvious disrespect for its past.

Backtracking to the marble marker, we wend our way counterclockwise along a mulched path bordered by pruned hedges. I pass the map to Martin, who turns it upside-down and scratches his head at the arrows and crosses and illegible words scrawled in black ink.

The western quadrant contains celebrity graves, maintained for tourists. The monuments are pockmarked by acid rain. Many of the crypts have diagonal cracks, their plaster walls having suffered damage during the Second World War.

Martin studies the epitaphs much as a visitor to an art museum might absorb information under random paintings. We trudge past a statue of Dostoevsky with a protruding stone beard.

Erik opens the umbrella and hands it to me. "I'll scout out the monastery," he says with a salute. "It's supposedly beyond the hedge."

Meanwhile, Martin has located Tchaikovsky and claps his hands with approval. Behind the bust, a massive, winged angel clasps a huge cross. A second angel sits reading on the grave itself. To our frustration, no brick mausoleum stands nearby. We follow the circular mulched track a second time. Return to Tchaikovsky.

"Damn! I promised my cousin Vania a photographic summary of our trip. Our great grandparents must be buried here somewhere. Everyone famous before the revolution is in this cemetery."

"Your relatives were famous?" Martin asks.

I do a slight wobble with my hand. "Famous enough."

Five minutes later, we meet up with Erik who gestures at an opening in the hedge. We cross a footbridge and enter the grounds of the Alexander Nevsky Monastery. Sentinel-like trees flank a paved lane, slick with fallen leaves. The sun emerges from behind a cloud, and shafts of light angle down on to the pavement. In the distance, a six-foot wall protects the monastery grounds from the city like the exoskeleton of a snail. A bearded man in clerical robes enters the church, its stucco walls pale yellow. On the steps, two janitors unroll a threadbare, wine-colored carpet. The monastery's bell tolls.

"Saint Nicholas," says Martin, raising his eyes from the guidebook. "If I'm not mistaken."

"Let's go in," Erik says.

"No! We need to keep searching. And there's a service going on."

"Exactly. It's an opportunity to witness Russian culture. Martin, you know the Bolsheviks banned religion, right? With perestroika, the government reversed the policy."

A wave of incense hits as we tiptoe past a wooden rack filled with lit prayer candles, which shimmer in the half-light. Candelabra hang from the vaulted ceiling. In the middle of the nave, several dozen worshippers bend their heads in prayer. A priest conducts the liturgy, and the faithful respond at appropriate intervals. The deep-throated voices of choir members add a solemn note to the service.

I stick close to Erik who has meandered halfway around the inside perimeter. He sidles into an empty spot near an alcove and goes into observation mode, arms crossed. At the opposite side of the nave, Martin follows suit, as rigid as an undercover agent in his beige raincoat. I let my mind wander to earlier in the day. Tires squealed as a thug drove his BMW onto the sidewalk, plowing into window shoppers, including a terrified babushka. A Mafia underling, executing orders, I concluded, or collecting protection money from the restaurant owner. My mind journeys on to Hotel Moscow and our lousy breakfast, open-faced bologna sandwiches, topped with a curl of sweet pickle. Not even a sweet roll worth filching for lunch. With its lumpy mattresses and plumbing fixtures from the fifties, our hotel barely deserved its three stars.

Erik's nudge ends my ennui. "Over there," he whispers. "It's your Mafioso."

In the middle of the worshippers stands the elegant man from the SAS passenger lounge, a votive candle in one hand. His gold wristwatch sparkles in the candlelight as he makes the sign of the cross. This time the ponytail fits right in with his pressed designer jeans, white T-shirt, and navy-blue blazer.

I'm meditating on how religion must have comforted my paternal grandparents after they lost their country when a barrel-chested man in a belted raincoat steps forward and whispers in Erik's ear.

"Sorry but I don't speak Russian," Erik says.

Alarm flashes across the stranger's face. He elbows his way through the worshippers and, with both arms, grabs the pony-tailed man, propelling him toward the exit. The votive candle rolls across the floor in their wake.

My imagination charges into high gear as Erik signals that we should follow. I can almost hear the machine guns ablaze and see the spotlights, like on a movie set, illuminating the ZIL-115 parked outside to whisk the men away.

To my relief, the lane is deserted except for a lone monk, hurrying past.

"I was counting on gangsters." I give a self-conscious laugh. "Maybe a bulletproof limousine."

"Someone has been reading too much James Bond."

I aim a playful punch at Erik's stomach. This second sighting of the man in the pale-yellow suit feels significant. In modern-day Russia, gangsters show up in church, accompanied by bodyguards. The St. Petersburg visit has made it abundantly clear that any attempt to recover real estate would be a waste of time. The deep sadness I experienced in the cemetery returns. The painters, plasterers, and carpenters in my mind give a sad wave and disappear into the mist.

We retrace our steps to the footbridge. Erik suggests dinner.

"Mind if I make a request first?" Martin asks.

"Be my guest," I say as we enter the cemetery.

"It's stopped raining. Why not play a tune for your ancestors?"

"Indeed," Eric says, a twinkle in his eye. "Do give us a concert."

After a moment of indecision, I open the violin case and ruefully show Martin the trowel cushioned on the velvet lining.

I glance around one last time and say a silent prayer for the souls of my great-grandparents, and another for the other "former people" crowded together in that wretched space, prominent aristocrats in their day whose lives have been reduced to a couple lines in a guidebook.

After dinner, we walk over to the Alexander Nevsky Bridge, where the city lights reflect off the water like millions of rubies.

The Courage It Takes

Kat Martello was having a particularly bad day. Her mom had died of cancer, leaving Kat and her three sisters to cope with Salvatore, who wasn't the most law-abiding citizen in New Jersey, far from it. Kat felt annoyed with her sisters Marina and Tasha at their inability to stop crying. Gabi had skipped town. And Kat was furious at their dad who had brought his new girlfriend to the funeral. Holy Redeemer was the wrong church for the service too. Add that to her list of grievances. Luba would have preferred Russian Orthodox, in Garfield. That's where this funeral should have taken place.

Kat shifted her shoulders against the pew. She felt all itchy in the black taffeta dress from Macy's that Aunt Daria had insisted she wear. Size 11, not 13. The other mourners had surely noticed. Kat recognized several kids from ninth grade, a few neighbors, her mom's former boss from the real estate office in Regency Park. She let her gaze fall upon Salvatore, crouched at the other side of the aisle, head down, so that all she could see was his stringy black hair combed back for once. Her dad was a big man, with plump slanting shoulders and padded sides. Seated beside him, Svetlana removed her gloves to reveal pointy fuchsia nails. She wore Luba's engagement ring, a heart-shaped diamond, rimmed with sapphires. How Kat loved that ring, not at all the girlfriend's style. As the mourners filed down the aisle to canned organ music, Salvatore made a show of holding out one arm for Svetlana to precede him. They headed toward the altar, where two shifty-eyed men jabbed their teeth with toothpicks.

Fingertips pressed to her temples, Kat spun around in the opposite direction. Frightful images flashed in on her at once: their mom's panicked expression after Gabi threatened to report Salvatore, his fists pounding on the door the night they took refuge in the bathroom, the tremble of Marina's chin, Gabi's belly laugh at realizing her sixteenth birthday present, a Chevrolet Caprice, provided a means of escape.

As Aunt Daria drew closer to the church exit, Kat sped up and poked her head outside. No sign of the Caprice with its distinctive black vinyl top. She gnawed the interior of her cheek, determined to appear unaffected by Gabi's decision to stay away. Sunday was Easter, a holiday Luba called the single most important day on the whole Orthodox calendar. Kat put her hand into a pocket and touched her laminated photo of Claire Danes as Angela in *My So-Called Life*. A light tap made her feel better.

Aunt Daria herded her nieces toward the rental car. She had parked in one of the two designated spots behind Salvatore's white Cadillac Eldorado. Tasha's tongue hung out as if she had been forced to swallow her pet canary. Kat hugged the vestibule wall, eyes peeled for Salvatore. She had decided to confront him about the ring.

"Katarina! What are you doing?" Daria shouted. "We're going to the cemetery."

"Not me," Kat said.

"Get in the car."

"She doesn't want to see Mommy being dumped in a hole," Marina said, eyes bloodshot. "Won't watch."

Tasha gave a shake to her braids, which Kat had tied with satin ribbons after breakfast. "I won't watch either. Let me out."

Before they could scramble from the backseat, their aunt slammed the passenger-side door and popped another tranquilizer. An angular woman, so different from Luba with her tidy figure, dark-eyed Daria was not the warm-and-fuzzy type. Their mom had appreciated her presence when the girls trooped through the hospital room for a final goodbye. Kat shuddered, summoning up Luba's wheeze and shortness of breath, the sweet, fruity smell of sickness, the head nurse's insistence that they break off their visit earlier than expected. That's what really set Daria off. It turned out she had plenty of sickbed experience, having tended to Aunt Babette, as well as to their grandmother. "Don't smoke," she snapped in the elevator. "Smoking leads to disease." Aunt Daria deserved a medal. Number one caregiver for cancer-ridden family members. A hapless job that received no credit. Kat decided she'd mention this too. Her plan was to confront the girlfriend first. That would be an effective way of shaming her father. She'd say, Hey, Svetlana. Did he tell you where he got that ring? Right off the finger of a dying woman. My mother. His amore. All she needed to do was approach. He wouldn't use violence in front of the parishioners.

Tasha's good-hearted second-grade teacher captured Kat's hand and clasped it to her bosom. By the time the woman released her, Kat had lost her nerve. Salvatore already stood at the bottom of the church steps. She watched him steer Svetlana toward the Cadillac, the most extravagant of his five vintage cars, reserved for special occasions. Under her breath, Kat cursed his "partner" who had introduced her parents.

Joey worked for the newspaper too. Kat had imagined the two men, proud members of the AFL-CIO, loading bundles onto delivery trucks until Gabi told her they signed up for different shifts because they punched the clock for each other, a ruse that resulted in halftime work for full-time pay and was proof of the criminal activity their mom had long denied.

On the walk home, Kat forced herself to think happy thoughts. Take the municipal park off to the right, for instance. Games of kickball with Gabi came to mind. How often Luba had taken them to the park in summer. She never failed to buy ice cream sandwiches from the Good Humor man.

Kat passed North Jersey Lanes. Her mom knew nothing about bowling, a sport that didn't exist in Europe. She never rolled anything but gutter balls and yet continued to insist on the Friday night bowling excursions. Kat liked to remember how Luba repeated, after each evening out, "Bowling is part of being American. You girls are little Americans. Not immigrants from Europe. Americans."

The Martellos had called the craftsman house on Elm Street home since 1982. A neighbor had left a basket of apples on the front porch. Kat unlocked the door and frowned at the living room. Her mom hated clutter. Tasha's nurse's costume and toy stethoscope lay on the slipcovered sofa, where she had changed her clothes. Oreo crumbs speckled the shag carpet, and Aunt Daria's Burberry travel bag remained open below the "Genghis Khan Leading the Mongols" poster that Salvatore had bought in a pawnshop after learning one of Luba's ancestors was married off to a Mongol invader in the thirteenth century.

Kat unzipped the taffeta dress and let the undergarment, a black crinoline, fall to the floor before giving a wanton kick to the pile of what Daria called *adequate funeral attire*. She opened the credenza drawer that contained the ultra-light Virginia Slims, forbidden by the oncologist. Knowing there would be consequences if all five packs disappeared, she hid four in the kitchen. Stretching her neck to remove the cricks, she grabbed an ice-cream sandwich from the freezer and headed for the shower.

*

Kat awaited her dad's return seated on the sofa with People Magazine across her lap. Aunt Daria sat beside her, removing nail polish with Luba's foul-smelling acetone from Europe. The VCR was hooked up to the television. Kat had muted the "Strangers in the House" episode of *My So-Called Life* in which Angela shows her inherent wisdom. She had taped the episode right before the show's cancelation. Standing in the kitchen doorframe, Luba had said appraisingly, "That brave girl doesn't let anyone get away with anything, does she?"

It didn't feel like Easter morning. There was no Russian Easter cheese, decorated with currants. No yeast bread, baked in Chock full o'Nuts cans. No cute candy chicks filled with marsh-mallow. No hard-boiled eggs dyed red with onionskins. And Daria kept asking all these stupid questions. Kat didn't want to talk about Gabi and she didn't want to talk about school and she certainly didn't want to talk about Salvatore. Figuring out what he would do next was like a game of Blind Man's Bluff, played in a minefield. It came as a relief when her aunt announced she had a plane to catch and packed her Burberry bag.

At the door Daria blew desperate kisses from cupped fin-gers. The look on her face indicated she was afraid she might never see her nieces again. "Luba loved you so much," she called from the curb. "Be good girls. Make your mom proud."

That afternoon, Kat got out the magic markers and told her sisters to list fun things to do over spring break. At the top of the page, she jotted down *Make buttered popcorn*. Tasha suggested Pick-up Sticks, Chinese Checkers, or decorating Easter eggs. Marina requested a fashion show, with makeup and sequins. The games ended after Tasha dumped a handful of popcorn kernels in her canary's cage, allowing the bird to escape. Kat vacuumed before bed lest her dad criticize. She knew he'd return. It was only a matter of time.

Sure enough, toward noon the next day, Salvatore came crashing through the mudroom, his Mets jacket draped over one shoulder, Svetlana at his elbow. It was disconcerting for Kat to realize she felt a certain relief. One lousy parent trumped being an orphan. She stood at the stove, intent on a batch of Aunt Jemima pancakes, and ignored the girlfriend, who coughed in the hope of acknowledgment. Smacking gum, Svetlana tottered on spiked heels, red like her parka, and peered expectantly across the threshold with the skittishness of a future tenant. Marina lay stomach-down on the sofa, legs bent at the knee, head buried in a comic book. With a playful shake of the finger, Salvatore tucked a strand of hair behind her ear, heroic in his Prince Charming persona. There. That ingratiating smile again. How could Luba have fallen for it? After Ouija board sessions with neighborhood girlfriends, Kat and Gabi had puzzled over their dad's personality in an attempt to understand why Luba had married him. They concluded he was the frog prince in reverse. Sharp looking, accommodating, and quick to compliment, pumped up with self-confidence.

"Then ladies, once hooked, watch out!" Gabi had said with scorn.

Kat couldn't help reminding herself of the good times. The Circle-line Cruise around Manhattan with both parents. The plush teddy bears from Coney Island. The gift of a gardenia corsage for Joey's restaurant opening in Margate, a couple of miles from the Atlantic City line.

Salvatore went straight to the refrigerator for a Diet Coke. From his clean-shaven cheeks, Kat could tell he wouldn't be staying. Indeed, he mounted the stairs two by two and descended a few minutes later with a duffel bag. She watched out of the corner of her eye, the way a herpetologist advised observing reptiles in a guidebook from the library. Back away slowly. Make no sudden gestures. Avoid contact if possible.

He laced his stubby fingers across his belt, worn below his belly, feet spread apart. "Who gave you permission to skip the cemetery? No respect for your mom, I see."

Kat raised one shoulder and let it fall back to indicate a lack of comprehension. She pointed the spatula at Svetlana, who was feathering her hair in front of the mudroom mirror. "Did Medusa go with you?"

"Watch your mouth, young lady. How about some appreciation for your old dad?"

At the Formica-topped kitchen table, Tasha concentrated on her pancake. She carefully sawed it in half with a plastic knife. Salvatore dropped a cemetery map on the table and tousled her blond hair. "Hey, Pumpkin. Gimme a kiss," he ordered.

As Tasha embraced him, Kat recalled having craved his attention at that age too.

Salvatore crushed the Diet Coke can down flat before jamming a one-hundred-dollar-bill into her peacoat pocket. He opened the hall closet and gave Svetlana Luba's sunglasses from Italy and her vintage bag with the intricate hinged top.

Kat groaned. What nerve. She needed to tell him this was thievery. She moved closer. "Dad, you really have no right to – "

"There's three of you 'til Gabriella gets back," he interrupted. "Kat babes, you're in charge."

Svetlana wiggled her fingers, a victory smile brightening her face. The couple sped off in her used Honda, Salvatore at the wheel. Tasha, who had finished lunch, imitated Svetlana's pigeon-toed walk. Kat and Marina burst into hysterical laughter. Laughter helped.

*

On Monday, Kat installed her sisters in front of the television and rode her bike to the cemetery. It was a clear day, with daffodils jackknifed by the stiff breeze. She trudged up Magnolia Avenue, scanning the inscriptions on graves. Cemeteries gave her the heebie-jeebies. She hoped there would be a decorative design in a corner of the headstone. Gardenias, maybe. Luba loved gardenias. As Kat stumbled through the mossy sod, she mulled over possible engravings for the headstone. *Beloved wife and mother*? Maybe not all that beloved. Esteemed wife and beloved mother. Sick wife and beloved mother. Abandoned wife and beloved mother. The school counselor had told her Salvatore didn't seem able to deal with illness, that his ambivalence was a method of coping.

The cemetery map proved useless. How was she supposed to find the gravesite? She surveyed all the neat headstones, read off the names as she passed by. Something shiny caught her eye in the downtrodden grass. She picked up Tasha's hair ribbon and felt a pang of anguish. Her mother was buried in an unmarked grave. To add insult to injury, the fresh mound of earth had no headstone. She hesitated, unsure what to do next. There was a pencil and a movie ticket stub in her pocket, perfect for jotting down names in order to locate Luba on future visits.

"I love you," she whispered. "Bye, Mommy."

Kat pedaled home feeling sorry for herself until she caught sight of the Caprice, parked at the end of the cul-de-sac. She snapped her fingers across the hood and quickened her step, relieved Gabi was back. The sisters would face the world better as a quartet.

Gabi wore thick black eyeliner, railroad-striped bib overalls, and the red bowling shirt Luba had bought last year, its pocket embroidered "Gabriella" in white cursive. She gave her characteristic two-finger salute from the sofa, one hand tickling Marina, who giggled quietly. Tasha, who sat on Gabi's lap, reached up to touch the spikey hair, now buzz cut and streaked blond. Gabi kissed Tasha's forehead and stood up. When she clamped her arms around Kat, she knocked some of the marbles from Chinese checkers to the floor.

Kat envied her brilliant elder sister, who now lived with relatives in New York. She had left home in a huff after Luba refused to let her call the police. It was a nightmare memory, one Kat sought to forget: the broken soup tureen, the bruised skin on Luba's wrist as she succeeded in wrenching the phone away, the whole episode conducted in whispers since Salvatore had been asleep upstairs.

"Mommy's gone," Kat said. She wanted to scream about the injustice of life but didn't. Luba had taught her to set a good example. Rectitude was required. Civility. Family allegiance.

"Where's Dad?" Gabi asked.

"He left with Svetlana." The thought made Kat roil with anger. If only she could muster the nerve to report him. The charge for abandonment might be more consequential than for abuse. "You missed the funeral."

"Yeah. On purpose."

Kat watched her sister carry her knapsack to the front hall and open the closet door. Luba's fuzzy spring coat still hung on a hook. Gabi embraced the coat, lifting the sleeve to her face to breathe in her mother's scent as Marina's giggles turned to sobs.

"Mom said to be strong," she scolded, pulling a shoebox off the closet shelf. "Stop your bawling, for Chrissake."

The Buster Brown shoebox contained Luba's photos. The 4x4s were faded and worn. Some had stuck together, stained by coffee. She held up a snapshot of Luba's childhood home. "Poor mom didn't know any better when she married you know who. I'd be willing to bet had she grown up here, never would she have gotten involved."

"He took her basket bag from Spain," Marina said.

"We can't let him get his hands on these." Gabi crammed the shoebox into her knapsack.

"There's no headstone," Kat said, shoulders hunched. She might as well have carried a piece of marble back from the cemetery to feel such immense fatigue.

"It's not simultaneous. Like you die and a headstone pops up on your grave? Is that what you think?" Gabi sounded indignant.

"Are they expensive?" Marina asked.

"I doubt it," Kat said, smarting at Gabi's tone. "And Dad's loaded."

"Ever wonder where he gets the cash for all those cars when he clocks so few hours?" Gabi flipped through a pile of mail and dumped most of it in the wastepaper basket. "Maybe he's ordered a headstone," she added, turning back to Marina. "Or maybe he hasn't. And, in that case, you can count on me. Mom's grave will have a headstone."

Marina made a heart with her fingers.

Kat said nothing. She twisted her mouth into a deep frown, in the hope of nudging Gabi away from a subject that Luba maintained should be raised on a need-to-know basis only.

"I'm off. Will you guys be okay?" Gabi surveyed her sisters as if they were baby birds with visibly broken wings. "You should know that I went to the hospital a couple days before Mom died. I promised I'd take care of you." At the front door, she drew in a sharp breath. "I can't for a while. But I will."

Kat kicked the base of the sofa. Gabi didn't intend to stay. Talk about injustice. She wanted to yell, *let me go with you* but hated the idea of leaving Marina and Tasha behind as jesters, with Svetlana as Salvatore's Queen of Hearts.

The Caprice backfired and disappeared down the street. Kat swallowed hard. How would she manage by herself?

*

Two weeks later, Salvatore hurtled through the mudroom preceded by a whiff of Aqua Velva. He took off his cap with its translucent visor and waved the souvenir, hopeful a trip to Florida would provide a legitimate excuse for his absence. Svetlana hovered in the doorway, which told Kat they had been on some perverted version of an early honeymoon. Her dad's fiancée was dressed in white slacks and sparkly sandals. She lit a Kool. Luba's Italian sunglasses dangled on a rhinestone chain around her neck.

Tasha threw her arms around Salvatore's waist. "Daddy, Daddy! You're back."

He kissed her and yelled up the stairs for Marina. Startled by his voice, the canary flapped down from its perch above the door, which made Svetlana let out a shriek of horror. Salvatore told Tasha he had carried home two awfully heavy conches for her shell collection. In the middle of describing the shell shop, his body language changed. Once he had taken in the full extent of the chaos—mud and bird droppings on the carpet, glitter on the table, magic marker on the slipcover, apple cores in his Mets ashtray, marbles scattered everywhere—a malevolent gleam sprang into his eyes. He gave his girlfriend a little shove.

"Sweetpea, back in the car. Go on now. Get going."

Svetlana followed orders, throwing nervous glances over her shoulder. As soon as she was out of earshot, Salvatore lurched across the living room. Kat didn't budge.

"Holy shit," he hissed, a foot or two away. His bushy eyebrows slanted down.

Kat stuck out her chin and braced for what was to come.

"I left you in charge of this family," he said, face flushed, and raised his voice several decibels until he was yelling. "How dare you do this to me?"

Tasha clapped her hands over her ears and pivoted toward the wall of knotted pine. "La-la-la-la," she sang.

Kat made a point of sizing up her father to let him know she wasn't intimidated. There was a story Luba used to tell. It was about a little girl and a pot of porridge that bubbled over because the villagers had forgotten the magic words required to make it stop. Luba had said something about finding the strength within oneself to end trauma. She was always carving life lessons out of fairy tales. All it had taken was the courage to say, "Little pot, stop." Otherwise, the village would have been overrun with porridge and the inhabitants would have died, smothered by breakfast.

"You rotten, no good –"

"Not much of a surprise with you as a dad," she taunted, hands on her hips.

"Katarina Marie, this is outrageous."

"Outrageous? I'll tell you what's outrageous. Your having left us alone. Your abandoning Mommy. Your carrying on with that . . . slut."

Salvatore swung his fist into the air and cut back down on a diagonal. Kat found herself on the floor, the air knocked out of her. Her wrist felt sprained. Her hip hurt too. The pain was excruciating.

Marina ran into the kitchen and tugged on Salvatore's arm. "Stop it!"

"Fuck off."

Kat opened her eyes to see Marina career toward the back door.

Salvatore leaned over Kat, presumably considering more violence, but changed his mind. He threw a wad of twenty-dollar bills over his shoulder as he strode out the door and down the flagstone walkway with Svetlana struggling to keep up.

*

Kat had never been inside the Clearview police station, a dilapidated clapboard building she had passed hundreds of times on her way to school. She limped over to the waist-high oak counter. A fist-sized decal of an officer's badge decorated the facade.

"Can I help you, hon?" the sergeant on duty said.

Kat ran her eyes over the metal file cabinets behind him. She had to raise her voice to be heard over the racket from the teletype machine and the speakers monitoring police cruisers. "I need to file a report."

"Okay but talk to the social worker first. Mrs. Jones should be back from lunch in a sec."

"Thanks," Kat murmured, hand in her peacoat pocket. She touched the Claire Danes photograph and fondled the cigarette she intended to smoke afterwards.

Soon a matronly woman hurried up the steps. The police sergeant told Kat to follow her. Mrs. Jones entered an office, bare except for a desk, a water cooler, and some lockers. She filled a Dixie Cup and pushed the door shut. It swung back open since the room was an add-on with a crooked floor covered with stained linoleum.

"Who did this to you, dear?"

At that moment Kat felt nothing could be worse than her current situation. Salvatore would not have knocked her down had Luba been alive. Who knew what he might do the next time she refused to obey orders? She took a couple sips of water. When she spoke, her voice was calm. "My dad hit me. My mom died of cancer three weeks ago, and he left with Svetlana. That's his new fiancée. He gave us money for food. He gave my mom's engagement ring to Svetlana before Mom died."

Her body clenched, wracked by silent sobs.

Mrs. Jones wrapped her arms around Kat, shooing away the police sergeant who stood in the doorway, fists curled in outrage.

Shamil

Alison Kleindahl rapped the knuckle on her index finger against the dashboard of her mother-in-law's 1965 Volvo Amazon and peered out the window at the desolate landscape surrounding the transfer station. Here's what she saw: a 6-foot chain-link security fence, low industrial-zone buildings, a flock of crane-like spotlights over the bulk disposal area, a few jagged outcroppings of rock in the distance, and a stretch of well-maintained RVs parked in a lot reserved for vacationers spending the day in downtown Strömstad. She was in Scandinavia with her husband to encourage his mom to de-clutter before her house went on the market. Norwegians with oil money offered big bucks for villas along the Swedish coast. The fisherman's cottage, with its water view, had become prime real estate in the five years since Alison met Vorontsov at a Mardi Gras masquerade party while on semester abroad. Disguised as Zelda, she had fallen right into the open arms of his F. Scott Fitzgerald and never looked back.

Nothing exciting ever happened during these periodic trips of theirs to Sweden. That day, silvery sunshine alternated with brisk showers. Another strenuous afternoon of moving furniture lay ahead. Alison didn't speak the language and was eager to resume her DEA in folk tales at the University of Paris III. She had explored all the major tourist attractions on previous visits: the town center with its Victorian fretwork, the island of Koster seven miles away, the stone ship in Blomsholm across the E6 highway. She yearned for something more exciting and decided her best bet was the outlet mall in Nordby, ten miles from the Norwegian border, where shops offered stylish clothing at cheaper prices than in Parisian boutiques. On second thought, that was a nonstarter. Vorontsov hated shopping.

What was taking him so long? It was a matter of simply paying for the annual card permitting bulk disposal. One Volvo station wagon after another drove up the access road, dragging metal trailers piled high with brush or construction waste. The dump was not the most important errand on her husband's to-do list. They still needed to swing by the library and pick up *The Memoirs of Roustam* for his dissertation.

A faded Mitsubishi sedan screeched on to the shoulder beside the windowless charity shed. Vorontsov had parked farther down, near the two-story administration building, catty-corner to five lime-green recycling receptacles, round like the bloated bellies of colossal garden elves, black rubber mouths open to receive sustenance. Alison stared at them absentmindedly, removed her glasses, located a lens-cleaning tissue in her purse. As she cleaned the lens, the elves seemed to wink at her.

She jabbed the glasses back on.

In the rearview mirror, she glimpsed two Middle Eastern immigrants ducking into the charity shed. The woman wore a flowered headscarf. Her bearded companion kept his head down. It was chilly for late June, which explained their parkas. The couple was probably accustomed to a warmer climate. It must be a challenge to adapt to a foreign country, especially now that Swedes were having second thoughts about the government's "open-our-hearts" policy in response to the Syrian civil war. One hundred and sixty-three thousand migrants had entered Sweden in 2015. The Moderate Party was unable to calm anti-immigrant sentiment voiced in private from Malmö in the south to Kiruna on the Arctic Circle.

Vorontsov's mom often griped about the situation: "What were they thinking? Where will the money come from to house and educate all these people?"

Had Mother-in-law forgotten the story of Grandfather Vorontsov's difficult journey in 1925 as a five-year-old refugee? His family had certainly struggled when they first arrived in Sweden with Nansen passports, having left all their possessions behind.

The immigrants climbed back into their car. The woman tucked in her ankle-length skirt before the Mitsubishi sped off. Alison might not have looked at the access road again if the sun hadn't emerged from under a cloud, sending a stream of sunbeams cartwheeling across the pavement and into the charity shed, where its reflection on metal caught her eye. She got out to investigate.

The shed's interior emitted a subtle bubble-gum scent. A naked light bulb dangled from a cord in the ceiling. She blinked a couple of times and lowered the hood on her rain jacket. The shed was almost empty, evidence of daily pickup by the efficient charity folks, but up on the top shelf lay what seemed to be a small sword. The immigrants must have discarded it. She sensed a presence and Vorontsov popped up at her elbow, back with an återvinningskortet, the magnetic card that would facilitate disposal of his mother's bulky tube television. He beckoned for her to follow him.

"Ronnie, wait," she said. "Somebody has left a sword."

"Oh, wow! That's not a sword."

"What do you call it?"

"A kindjal. I've always dreamt of owning one."

He patted both cheeks with joy before lifting the shiny object off the shelf. Vintage weapons made him ridiculously happy. Yes, there was that familiar toothy grin. Last spring, he had brought home a Caucasian saber from the Porte de Clignancourt flea market. The shashka hung on the wall in their studio.

On a recent BBC *Antiques Roadshow*, a schoolteacher had requested the appraisal of a Caucasian dagger, inherited from an uncle who taught ancient history at Oxford. This weapon seemed more intimidating. It was two feet long, straight, and tapered into a sharp point, with a single groove on either side of the blade. Skill had gone into the fashioning of the silver scabbard. A green gemstone was embedded in both hilt and pommel. Two tassels hung from a silken braid, its threads silver, black, and red.

Vorontsov and Alison exchanged conspiratorial winks. She peeked outside. A dump employee sorted glass bottles and beer cans under the blue and white Strömstad Municipality flag, but otherwise the recycling area was deserted. No sign of the charity volunteers or their truck.

Before Alison had a chance to say finders-keepers, Vorontsov slid the kindjal from its scabbard. The wind picked up. Cement dust swirled. The kindjal and scabbard flew out of his hands and clattered to the floor. The air took on a sour tang. It smelled like someone had been boiling sweaty tennis shoes. There was a flash of light, and what seemed to be a person appeared brandishing a dagger, blade down. Two ornate three-pronged candelabra wobbled into place on either side. Its candles flickered.

"I am Shamil," he said in an imperious voice. "Shariah law I enforce with fire and sword."

The stranger stood motionless, shoulders back, with the self-importance of a celebrity, boots planted apart. He reminded Alison of Bob Barker on *Truth or Consequences*, which she used to watch as a child at her grandmother's house, only this man carried the weight of anger on his shoulders. He was bearded and wore a tall lambskin cap. Silver lacework trimmed his black tunic. Across his chest, double rows of cartridge cases.

"The Lion of Daghestan!" Vorontsov exclaimed.

"Who?"

"That famous freedom fighter I told you about. The religious leader who tried to unite Caucasian tribes."

"Whoa! I bet he's come for his sword."

"Kind-jal."

"Whatever."

"You wanted excitement, darling. You've got it."

Slit eyes fixed them with a terrible gaze that evoked windy nights and the forlorn mountaintops crested with fresh snow in one of Vorontsov's reference books. Alison kept an appearance of calm, though it was rather unsettling to encounter a nineteenth-century freedom fighter with dirt under his fingernails. She reached into her back pocket for her iPhone and made a face because she had left it on her mother-in-law's kitchen sofa.

"May Allah be praised for having sent me to lead Muslims against the Infidel," Shamil said. His voice had a distinct high quality as if each word was precious and he didn't want to use too many at a time. He flexed his knees, stiff from confinement.

Alison opened her mouth to tell him Swedes were compassionate souls—the government had only closed the borders once the social welfare system became overloaded—but she didn't have the courage to speak. He wasn't the type of person you could contradict.

Shamil scooped up the kindjal with his right hand, stained the dark orange of henna like his beard, and switched into Arabic, mentioning Allah several times in the same sentence. Vorontsov unbuttoned his shirt pocket, took out the pad he used to jot down points to develop in his thesis, and unhooked a stubby pencil.

"Don't take notes," Alison said, aghast. "Do something!"

Meanwhile, their companion had overcome his initial disorientation because he now strutted up and down with a predatory gait, eying the doorway, presumably ready to bound into the countryside and champion the immigrants of Middle Eastern descent who had already found asylum in Sweden: Kurds, Iraqis, Iranians, Afghanis. He pointed the kindjal past the recycling receptacles toward a ledge of stone that jutted out of the landscape, threw back his head, and indulged in a full-throated laugh.

Alison summoned to mind her coursework on Scandinavian folklore. Trolls were supposed to be short creatures, capable of shapeshifting. They hid in stony outcroppings or mountains and feared sunlight, except for Olog-Hai. Could Shamil be a troll in disguise? He showed no sign of needing to stay inside the shed, so she doubted vulnerability to sunlight would pose a problem.

Or maybe he was a djinn. According to the Quran, Allah created djinns from smokeless fire. They possessed broad powers, which explained how he happened to speak English.

She had a hunch what needed to be done—send him back from whence he came—and whispered this in Vorontsov's ear. The reverse magic probably involved either the kindjal or the scabbard. It was unlikely a djinn would leave of its own accord.

Evidently having read her mind, Shamil chopped the air with his dagger to demonstrate intransigence and spoke a few succinct words in Arabic. Bushy eyebrows drew together in anger. Now, he was waving the kindjal over his head. He severed the electric cord with one pass of the weapon. The light bulb hit the floor and shattered. He swung the kindjal around, angled in, and thrust the tip at Vorontsov's cheek and back, drawing pearls of blood. Her jaw dropped.

"Oh, God, honey. Are you okay?"

She kept a couple Band-Aids in her purse, just in case. Hands shaking, she peeled one open, eyes on Shamil, who posed more of a threat than first imagined. His dexterity with knives made her fear for their lives.

To her horror, he was drawing circles in the air in her direction. "No hijab, woman? For shame."

She shot him a polite scowl and raised the hood on her rain jacket. "Do something, Ronnie," she muttered. "You're the one with all the bright ideas."

Vorontsov picked up the scabbard and extended his other hand, slow and steady. "That's some kindjal you've got there. Mind if I take a closer look?"

Shamil hesitated. He seemed to weigh the consequences.

"I have a shashka myself. If you'd like to see it, I can show you."

Vorontsov grabbed his iPhone from his jeans pocket. He scrolled through to the photos of their studio, taken for his mother, too ill to travel to France.

Shamil leaned over and stared at the Caucasian saber.

When he relinquished his weapon, it was with the pride of ownership and a desire to share a prized possession with someone who appreciates great workmanship.

In no time, Vorontsov had replaced the kindjal in its scabbard. The shed shook with what sounded like a clap of thunder. The candles guttered and the candelabra disappeared. In the blink of an eye, Alison and Vorontsov found themselves alone again.

*

They took the kindjal back with them to Paris. Alison had wrapped the lower third in electrical tape as a precaution. She suggested donating the weapon to the Institut du Monde Arabe, but Vorontsov convinced her the Musée Guimet should be their first choice. Before leaving home, she cut off one of the tassels as a souvenir, and Vorontsov took a selfie, holding the kindjal the way Shamil was wont to do in photos, halfway down the scabbard. They kept mum about his appearance in the charity shed. Alison did specify, however, that their gift should always be sheathed.

The curator assured them that vintage weapons receive the respect they deserve and remain in their original condition. No polish, no alteration. He labeled the glass case, *Caucasian kindjal in its scabbard, believed similar to the kindjal belonging to the great warrior Shamil and used in the Murid war, 1830-1849.*

The tassel adorned their mirror for years. When late afternoon sunshine crossed their studio on the Rue de la Victoire, the silver threads shimmered as if to remind Vorontsov of their provenance, as if dreams really did come true.

The Pilgrimage

Toward the end of January, I drove my Volkswagen beetle Cucaracha out to Charles de Gaulle Airport to pick up Katarina Martello. Luba's lanky second daughter emerged from customs wide-eyed and jetlagged. If I were obliged to describe her on paper to individuals at the Missing Persons Bureau, I'd write that she resembled a normal teenager, as normal as they come, more attractive than most, with pale freckled skin and lustrous chestnut hair, the type of hair featured in shampoo commercials.

"Welcome, Katarina!" I gave her a loose hug. "We're going to have so much fun together."

"People call me Kat."

She spoke in a high-pitched voice, her oversized make-up case balanced on the edge of the baggage carousel. An uncomfortable silence stretched between us as she slipped a slender hand into her pocket for a pack of cigarettes. The girl was nervous. Not surprising. First passport. First trip to Europe. First meeting with a distant cousin who might send you back to foster care if you misbehaved.

The instant our eyes met my brain summoned up her mother. My beloved pen pal Luba Martello had ended our correspondence in 1975, the year Salvatore got her pregnant and destiny launched us in opposite directions. Straight out of Georgetown's School of Foreign Service, I landed a job at the American Consulate in Barcelona while Luba found herself in

Queens, New York, having married into an Italian American family. I dismissed the rumors of abuse, unwilling to believe anyone could harm such a sweet soul. Our paths continued to diverge until 1995 when her sister Daria called to say Luba had died of cancer. I sent her children—four daughters—my condolences. That fall, I took Gabriella, her eldest, out to dinner. I tried not to stare at the gold ring in her nose and kept the conversation off sensitive subjects, only letting my guard down when we parted company with a promise to make myself available should she ever need assistance. Gabriella's Christmas card two years later confirmed my worst fears: *After Mom died, Dad dropped off $100 for food and disappeared for a week. He told Kat to take care of our sisters. When she talked back, he knocked her black and blue. Now she's in foster care. The foster mom treats her like a permanent babysitter. The other fosters keep trying to set the house on fire. She'll be eighteen soon. You've got to save my sister.*

By the time I received this SOS, I had finished subsequent years in Madrid and been reassigned to Paris. I placed several calls to Social Services and orchestrated a trip to Europe with unused airline miles. Four months: February, March, April, May. I could certainly manage four months. In June, I'd put her back on a plane and Gabriella could take over.

I collected Katarina's thirty-inch wheelie-bag from the carousel. The black fabric featured jet planes, London bridges, Eiffel towers, and lip imprints—both red and hot pink—as well as come-ons: *Date me; Hi, sweetie; Ooh, la la.*

Off we went, direction Paris.

I had run out of small talk by the time Cucaracha eased into its reserved spot behind a four-story building in

Rueil-Malmaison, the French town I've called home since scoring the Embassy job. Marble lobby, concierge service, modern conveniences, easy access to the former home of Empress Josephine. And glory be, Providence provided American neighbors whose kids attended an international school nearby, an ideal means of meeting other young people for my houseguest.

Katarina—Kat—picked at her cuticles in the elevator. To lessen her anxiety, I went straight to the guestroom, decorated in black and white. Nothing fancy, except my trophy wall. I stated the rules while we admired the completed jigsaw puzzles of Parisian landmarks: the Eiffel Tower, Sacré Coeur, Place Vendome.

"One: no smoking, especially in my new Volkswagen. Two: use tissues, not washcloths, to remove your makeup. Three: there's a midnight curfew. I leave for the Embassy at eight Monday through Friday. My only weekend commitment is Sunday school at the Unitarian Church near Bastille."

She remained mute. Unsure what more to say, I produced her mother's letters, mailed in the sixties, and turned on my heel.

By the end of the weekend, I had bought a Carte Orange pass, demonstrated how to use the RER regional subway, and made a deposit on classes at l'Alliance Française.

"Your mom would have wanted you to learn the language," I reminded her when she overslept, missing class. But Kat gave up on the French lessons a couple of weeks in. I suggested movies, museums, a tour of the city by Bateau Mouche. She politely declined. With all of Paris to discover, she spent her days moping around the apartment, homesick for a boyfriend named Buddy, a Harley Davidson devotee she had met over New Year's.

When I peeked into the guestroom after work, she would be folding clothes into neat piles: T-shirts, thongs, bras, short shorts, dresses. I found the habit strange until she explained her high school offered mall training for credit since most teenagers in Clearview, New Jersey, end up in retail. The monotony helped her "chill."

Once, home early, I found her playing solitaire with my Expo–92 cards. She tucked the deck back into its box. Her fingers floated to her earrings, eyes avoiding mine. "Buddy called. He's opening a restaurant. Could I, like maybe, help you with dinner?"

That was the start of our cooking extravaganza. I taught her apple tart and cauliflower au gratin and beef Bourguignon. She taught me s'mores, replacing graham crackers with Petit Beurres, a substitution recommended by the neighbor's daughter, Bethany. Gradually we settled into a rhythm that seemed to work for both of us.

In mid-February, Kat mentioned Bethany had dropped out of school first semester with mono. The two girls had started spending time together. Soon they were barhopping on weekends. While this activity didn't exactly make me rejoice, at least Kat had won her battle with homesickness. I felt ready to applaud any victory, no matter how insignificant.

Our life proceeded without incident for another month. The crisis arose in late March. She had gone out Saturday night, dressed in her fanciest get-up—daisy shorts and black tights, white T-shirt, black leather thrift-shop jacket—and missed curfew. Bethany's mom urged patience, forbearance, faith in our girls' sense of right and wrong. We exchanged more phone calls, discussed alerting the police. Meanwhile, I imagined various scenarios. Kat and Bethany had been mugged. They lay in a dark Parisian alley, no doubt unconscious. Or, worse, kidnapped by human traffickers, they were halfway to Marrakesh, destined to live out their lives in a North African harem. I tried my best to work on the jigsaw puzzle of the Pompidou Center, which had arrived in the afternoon mail, but concentration proved elusive. I paced the hallway, brewed several teapots of Earl Grey. By the time Kat turned the key in the lock, it was 3 a.m.

I convinced myself not to scold, attributing the incident to Bethany's influence. I smoked a furtive Benson & Hedges on the balcony and pondered how to make a difference in Kat's life. Luba's sister Daria had invited her niece to Geneva for a visit. I planned to take time off to drive her there. Why not stop on the way and visit Luba's childhood home, a renovated mill at the foot of the Jura mountains? Perhaps Kat needed to connect with her mother's past. Perhaps the mill would work its magic on my houseguest, the way it had on me.

*

Luba was born in White Plains, New York. Her father, a simultaneous interpreter at the United Nations, accepted a similar job in Geneva and bought a half-acre of land across the French border. The property included two dilapidated structures. Once renovation of the millhouse was complete, Luba's parents took in boarders.

At seventeen, I spent three weeks as a member of their household. The memories remained so fresh: the train streaking into Cornavin Station, where billboards advertised Lindt chocolate and Mövenpick ice cream; my fear of not finding Aunt Katia in the crowd of strangers; her hospitality that made me feel so welcome.

Aunt Katia drove an odd-shaped, lollopy vehicle called a Deux Chevaux, which swayed along narrow back roads until we reached Bes, population twenty-five. She parked below a two-story stucco building with turquoise shutters and palmed the horn. White muslin curtains billowed from first-floor windows as if the millhouse were a swan, flexing its wings, about to fly away.

To the west rose the teal blue Juras, peaked with snow. I grabbed my Instamatic and snapped a photo of a telephone tower halfway up the closest mountain. When I swung around to capture the millhouse, Aunt Katia's three daughters raced through the gate, flapping around us like exotic butterflies. Exuberant French words flew at me from all directions.

"I'm so happy to be in Bees," I said after introductions.

The eldest cousin burst out laughing. Daria wore black-framed cat's eye eyeglasses which kept sliding down her nose. "Not like the insects. Short letter E. It's pronounced Beze."

Luba, the middle cousin, looped her arm through mine and shot me a tender look. Her sisters followed as we made our way up a concrete walkway into the front yard, delineated by a hand-sawed picket fence. Luba showed off the walkway's treasures: a sunburst marble, shards of Delft pottery, an Indian head charm from a Cracker Jack box. Three handprints memorialized the artists.

"Papa poured," Daria said.

"We helped," Babette, the youngest cousin, added in French.

"Wrong," Daria scoffed. "You dawdled. I worked."

An eight-foot retaining wall framed the garden's eastern rim. The girls explained how their dad had diverted the mill-stream so that it would flow through a stone basin built into the fieldstone wall. Raised in cities—Chicago, Boston, Seattle—I asked about the presence of a fountain, afraid it would keep me awake.

"People sleep well here," Luba replied.

"It's the mountain air," added Babette.

Next, they showed off their "American" swimming pool, a nightmare do-it-yourself project if ever there was one. Daria admitted the pool had not seen much use due to the unantici-pated expense of chemicals. Leaves floated on the surface of the murky water, a reminder that dreams can be thwarted by circumstance.

That first morning, we ate breakfast at a picnic table under a cherry tree. The smell of fresh coffee wafted through the air, mixed with the scent of clove from purple stock and a jumble of petunias. I slipped onto the bench beside Luba who gave my forearm two quick love taps before meeting Daria's gaze. Hands-off, Luba's eyes said. I was in France as an English-speaking companion for her sister, closest in age at fifteen, but thirteen-year-old Luba had disrupted this plan, claiming me like some prize, a great book that would open her eyes to an America the three sisters dreamed of, a mythical land across the sea where money grows on trees, and everyone drives a Cadillac.

Babette squeezed in beside me, encircling my waist with both arms. Luba pushed her away.

"Pest! Leave our guest alone!" shrieked Daria from across the jars of homemade jam.

Luba grasped my hand, and we fled up the slope behind the millhouse. A hayfield extended in a plateau toward the horizon. The location offered front-row seats for the ballet of tiny Swiss Air jets landing in Geneva. Luba sank into the tall grass and laughed, a spontaneous giggle that bubbled up from inside her like the stream her father had diverted. Clasping her side, she allowed her body to fall back into the freshly mown hay. The air sparkled with our complicity.

We escaped to that hayfield often. Luba liked to bring *Introduction to Palmistry,* a book left behind by a British boarder. Heads together, we studied each other's palms, attempting to read the lines—life, head, heart, destiny. The squiggles under her pinky predicted three children.

"If anything should happen to me, promise you'll watch over those children," she said that day. "Promise!"

*

Paris/Geneva requires six hours by car. After leaving the A6 motorway, Cucaracha climbed the hairpin curves that led to a mountain pass. I stopped the car so Katarina could admire the view: tiled rooftops, conifers, the occasional church steeple. We drove on, past a corroded road sign for the nearest border crossing.

"Your mom helped me learn French in a hayfield," I said. "Her parents took in boarders to supplement their income."

"Like, you came all this way to learn a language?"

Although I was proud of my French proficiency, my sojourn in Bes had represented much more than a linguistic experience. Her wise-guy attitude made me exult in regaining my privacy for the two weeks she would spend in Daria's care.

Kat didn't want to talk. Fine! Perhaps I had been too pushy? But, as soon as I stopped seeking contact, she became loquacious. We chatted about the lack of fast food on the French highway, boyfriends, the weather, the fluffy clouds on the eastern side of the Juras that day. As Cucaracha wound its way down the mountain, I sensed a gradual change in her body language. She relaxed with each mile that brought us closer to destination.

The ground flattened out and we veered south on a two-lane country road.

"In my humble opinion, this trip is taking way too long," she said.

"Only a few more miles."

"You cool with me lighting up?"

"Can't it wait?"

I regretted my no-cigarettes-in-the-car rule when she started attacking her cuticles in that compulsive way of hers. Those hands were so like Luba's. Fine-boned hands, with perfect oval nails.

"Do you know where your mom's parents were born?"

"What's this? A quiz?"

"Where in Russia?"

"Beats me."

"St. Petersburg."

"Called Leningrad until a year or two ago. Dad's girlfriend is from Leningrad."

I glanced over to judge her reaction to Salvatore's having a girlfriend. She had said these words with no more emotion than would be required to read a shopping list. Gabriella had told me their father had given Luba's engagement ring to a woman he started dating while their mother was in the hospital.

"Did you know Daria took your granddad to his childhood home before he died?"

"De-dush-ka," she said, pronouncing the Russian word for grandfather with care. "He brought us chocolate lollipops when he visited Clearview. I was six."

"The Soviet government turned his family's townhouse into a museum. Guess what happened. The doorman recognized your granddad. All those years later. Hugged him."

"Must have been freaking old."

People get old I want to tell her. Then they die. The memories are all that remain.

*

My heartbeat accelerated as the landscape assumed the familiar contours of the hamlet where Luba spent her childhood. In the sixties, there had been a real farm in Bes, with black and white cows that mooed as they ambled past. Cowbells rang at dawn and in late afternoon, making bellies rumble in anticipation of the evening meal, sweet punctuation to each day.

We coasted along until the road snaked into a limestone village. With all this business of searching the landscape for cows, I had missed the turn-off. Orange roof tiles sparkled atop low gray buildings. Disgruntled, I parked in front of a café.

Kat had taken out a Walkman. Her head bobbed in time to the beat. "What are you listening to?" I shouted.

"The Velvets." She lifted a foam headset off one ear. "Buddy loves the Velvet Underground."

I shook the car key toward the post office, across the street. "This is where your mom mailed those letters. We're stopping here for coffee."

Kat rewarded me with a yawn.

"Her letters were postmarked right here," I insisted, surprised at how vivid the memory of an insignificant detail could be.

From her pocket, Kat drew the packet of frayed envelopes. I peered down at Luba's meticulous handwriting, practiced on graph paper until she got the cursive letters right, and it occurred to me that second grade in a French village could not have been the only cultural challenge she faced after being uprooted from White Plains, New York.

Kat removed the flimsy headset to order freshly squeezed orange juice and a chocolate croissant. I ordered an espresso as she headed off toward a door marked WC, her makeup case clutched to her breast with the devotion corgi owners afford their pet.

Dreadful rumors about her mom's life flooded back. When I succeeded in reaching Luba over the phone, she had answered my questions in monosyllables. I puzzled over her transformation and entertained the idea of an impromptu visit. That didn't happen though. Daria had warned me about Salvatore.

Kat returned with a fresh copy of Paris Match, the magazine cover filled with Madonna's sleek profile. The headline read "The Truth About Her Daughter's Father: The Shocking Interview."

"It was in the trash," she said, presumably sensing disapproval, and stuffed the magazine into her shoulder bag.

I decided to seize what might be one of my last opportunities to learn more about Luba's life. "Did you know I called your mom once or twice when you were a child?"

"Yeah. You said that."

"She didn't want to talk to me."

"Get out of here. I'm sure she would have wanted to talk to you." Kat dropped her eyes and twisted a strand of hair around her finger.

Red flags were waving but I forged ahead regardless.

"She used to speak to her sisters in French or Russian. I heard your dad made her speak English over the phone and listened in on every conversation."

She paused to evaluate the consequences of confirming what might have passed for a rumor. "Sounds about right," she said as the shopkeeper stepped up to our table with orange juice, croissant, and hot coffee. "Dad's a total control freak."

I feared she would shut me out, that our conversation would end there, but on the contrary, I learned a few more details of what must have been Luba's hell: "Hate that smell. When Mom was in the hospital, if his coffee wasn't hot enough, he'd throw it at me."

I stared at her, speechless. Before I could mention the unacceptability of lobbing a cup of coffee at anyone, she asked about her mother's name. I told her Luba was a nickname for Liubov', that, in Russian, Liubov' means love.

"Lulu is what he called her," she said with a snort of indignation and replaced the headset.

*

We drove back up the road, determined to find the turn-off. I downshifted and Cucaracha advanced at a crawl. To the left, a housing development. To the right, a shopping mall. We crossed the lower third of what must have once been Luba's hayfield. Instead of Holsteins, there were modern bungalows, surrounded by wide yards with shoulder-high hedges. I gazed up at the teal blue mountains and located the telephone tower. Her hamlet had to be nearby.

"Their school bus stopped here."

Kat sat up a little straighter. "Are we close?"

"Speak, memory," I muttered. "Help us find the mill."

Farther along, an abandoned road branched off at an obtuse angle. The rusty sign, toppled at some point, had been easy to miss. I got out to read it: *Bes, 1.*

Kat stuck her hands into her Hi Sweetie makeup case and lifted out the Buster Brown shoebox Gabriella had shown me. It contained Luba's photo collection.

"Mom liked to share her memories of the mill. She'd get tears in her eyes," Kat said, as if most housewives kept their life in a box. "Guess this place was pretty important to her, huh?"

On cue, the mill rose, majestic, more like a Tuscan palace than an old house in rural France. The new owners had painted the walls ochre. Honeysuckle cascaded over what remained of the picket fence.

Kat busied herself reviewing photos, snapping each one down methodically. She clicked her tongue in victory at a specific image, lifted the photo into her line of vision, and shaded her face as a blast of sunlight pierced the cloud cover, illuminating the millhouse. Her eyes danced back and forth until the corners of her mouth turned up in a half-smile.

We ascended the familiar walkway. The heavy oak door had no buzzer, so we knocked. Head to one side, she touched the façade the way a child might to detect a heartbeat.

"Yeah. Like in the picture." With a nervous laugh, she stuck a Marlboro between her lips. Her hands were shaking so hard it took a while to light.

I tilted my head at the retention wall, now covered with moss. A couple of empty flowerpots filled the stone basin.

"There was a fountain in this wall. It gurgled at night."

"Huh?"

"Made noise. Water, falling into the basin. Spring water. We drank it. See this stone basin? There was a stream up in the woods. The falling water turned the millstone. We loved the sound."

"Mom drank water from a spring. How gross."

"Your mom and her sisters were industrious. They dug themselves a swimming pool."

I made my way through the bumpy sod to the rear of the building with Kat trailing close behind. The owners had filled the pool with dirt.

We retraced our steps to the front door.

Our next stop was the cherry tree, cracked in places and bent over like the decrepit uncle in Gogol's *Dead Souls*. Someone had amputated major limbs. The picnic table was gone too.

"Your granddad's colleagues from the United Nations came here on weekends."

Their chatter rang out, cheerful voices speaking a variety of languages. In my mind, I sat at an improvised "children's table" in the dining room while Aunt Katia and Uncle Kolia entertained guests, White Russians, like most of their friends and acquaintances. Our family coat of arms—two crossed swords, a boat, an anchor, a spur—hung above the samovar, which shimmered in the candlelight.

"It wasn't what the adults said at those dinners, but what was left unsaid. That we belonged to the same tribe, a tribe that had suffered reverses. The Bolshevik Revolution might have decimated the aristocracy, but those who survived held their head high."

I ended my monologue with an unintentional sob.

Kat didn't hear a word of it because she had wandered back to the front door and was eying a decorative alcove, set high in the wall, the perfect hiding place for a door key. On tiptoe, she tried to reach inside. Perhaps my expectations were also out of reach. I had hoped to inspire her with pride in her Russian ancestors.

"Oh, shit! Broke a nail," she said and slapped stucco from her hands.

"Shall we go see the hayfield before we leave?"

Kat gave her head a resolute shake. She took one last drag on the cigarette and crushed the butt with a high heel, batting the air to disperse the smoke. As an afterthought, she bent down to examine the walkway. It didn't take long to find her mother's handprint. With a halting gasp of recognition, she knelt in the grass, palm pressed to the cold concrete.

Later that day, I would drop her in Geneva with Daria, who still favored cat-eye eyeglasses but wore a designer brand. She had gained weight but not much. Kat rolled her eyes during the demonstration of how to make a bed—smooth out bottom sheet, create a 45-degree angle with top sheet, tuck in. She frowned at mention of a nine o'clock curfew and clung to me before I climbed into Cucaracha, making my heart seize up as I drove away.

But right now, I watch Kat's hand linger on Luba's handprint and feel at one with the universe.

"Thanks," she said softly. "It feels good to know where Mom came from."

I too felt grateful. Katarina had given me the opportunity to do one last good thing for her mother. And, I felt lighter, as if a burden had been lifted.

Acknowledgements

The Nansen Factor begins with a story my father Paul Grabbe outlined in the 1920s, after his arrival in Colorado as a refugee, which I subsequently fictionalized as "The Errand."

I wrote most of these stories while taking courses at GrubStreet in Boston. Several teachers offered encouragement including Chip Cheek, Christina McCarroll, KL Pereira, Courtney Sender, and Dariel Suarez. Thank you!

Michael Mogilevsky shared facts about his mother's decision to live in Shanghai and allowed me to write a story based around those facts, creating a heroine who was not his mom but who survived similar displacement.

Dr. D—Natalie de Leuchtenberg Bowers—inspired "La Petite Boche."

Alexandra Kalinine described the challenges her relatives faced, which went into my crafting of "The Horror of It All."

Gavin Keenan helped me imagine the police station scene in "The Courage It Takes."

I'd like to express appreciation to Alexander Vassiliev, author of *Beauty in Exile*, a book which provides a clear idea of what life was like, after emigration, for members of the Russian nobility who influenced the world of fashion.

Nick Grabbe and Betsy Krogh read early drafts. Thanks also go out to readers Stephanie Boutin, Catherine Cole Janonis, Meredith Wadley, and proofreader Carolyn White Lesieur.

Whitney Scharer created the cover design. Steffen Thalemann contributed the photo. Gina Panettieri guided final steps.

Thank you to Sven Rudstrom for his patience as I wrote and rewrote these pages. He kept guard over the home front while I traveled to Boston for class. When I told him I was a writer in 1988, he commented on how difficult it is for writers to sell their work. But he believed in me and now, 36 years later, here's the result.

I dedicate these stories to my Russian relatives in France who welcomed me as a teenager and shared their hopes and dreams.

Thank you to Yelena Lembersky for suggesting I contact Cherry Orchard Books, to Alessandra Anzani for her enthusiastic support, and to the whole team at Academic Studies Press including Maria Gargyants, Daniel Frese, Matthew Charlton, and Becca Kearns.

At a time when mass migration and displacement is again plaguing the world, it's worthwhile to remember that changing countries and nationalities is hard and leaves scars.

Printed in the USA
CPSIA information can be obtained
at www.ICGtesting.com
JSHW080746190524
63366JS00002B/6